TRAIL
FROM
NEW ORLEANS
TO SANTA FE

JIM EDD WARNER

ISBN: 979-8-9865029-2-2 (Paperback)

Cover designer: GetCovers
Graphic designer: Deborah Stocco

For my Family,
Stacey, Travis, Tyler, Juliana, Charlotte and Henry

TABLE OF CONTENTS

ACKNOWLEDGMENTS

My wife Stacey Warner and sons Travis and Tyler and our friend Barb Hayter have all been helpful and encouraging in the writing of this book. I would also like to thank Diane Payne for help in editing this book.

1 | HEADING TO SANTA FE

My horse, Morgan, was giving it all he had and thank goodness it was enough. Several minutes before, I felt one of the arrows from an Indian hunting party plant itself in the rear of my saddle, just an inch or so below my lower back. It was a California style saddle that my brother, Troy Rampy, had bought from a vaquero in Mexico several years before. I got the saddle from him when he decided to go into the dry goods business in New Orleans. He gave it to me on one condition. He wanted me to go across-country to Santa Fe and try to round up some trading business for the both of us. I was beginning to doubt the arrangement at the moment.

There was no wind. The ground was flat and the land was wide open, so Morgan and I had an advantage. I would have been in real trouble if the small band of Kiowa I stumbled into hadn't been as surprised as I was. Like me, they had been hunting when they ran into an "intruder" in their territory. They took chase, but fear had gotten me to moving faster than them. Their ponies were fresh and would have been more than a match for Morgan if they had found us on hilly ground. But on wide open flat land like this, Morgan could run faster than any horse I had ever ridden.

The cries of the Kiowa faded into the distance, allowing me to slow to a trot, and then to a stop as I crested a small rise. I was fairly certain at this point that the Kiowa had given up the chase and returned to their hunt. After all, they had done what they wanted to do by running me off their hunting grounds. It was likely though that I had not seen the last of the Kiowa. They were supposedly scattered all through the area in front of me as I headed west. I was intending to follow the path of the Red River, but I wanted to stay far enough away from the river to avoid the Kiowa, Apache, Comanche, and Wichita. They apparently all used the river as a source of water and game.

As the sun was getting lower in the sky, on what had turned out to be a gorgeous summer day, I thought it prudent to look for a place to bed down for the night. I soon found a narrow valley that promised water, and hopefully cover, as I moved toward the river.

In the valley, I came across several vultures scavenging a deer carcass. What was left of the deer appeared to have been young and healthy, so I had to assume it had been killed by a large predatory animal. The largest predator in this area was a mystery to me. I knew that farther west I might run into mountain lions. As far as I knew, I was still several hundred miles away from anything that could be called a mountain. It was clear, however, that I would need to be careful. A mountain lion was nothing to mess with. Even in the daylight, and from a distance, I wouldn't challenge one. Close-up in the dark I wouldn't have much of a chance.

I decided to stop for the night near a small spring. I picketed Morgan with a lightweight rope, so that he could get both water and grass. After circling our camp in a wide arc on foot to assure we were alone, I unsaddled and brushed Morgan. Then I settled down by my saddle and had a little dried bread and meat. As was my custom, until it was too dark, I would read. I had brought several books and a few other papers with me. That evening I had reviewed a paper on the legal system of the new state of Alabama. It was where I grew up and where I always figured I would return someday to practice law. However, Troy had other ideas for me and himself.

Troy wanted the two of us to start our own trading empire. That didn't sound too bad to me, and I liked adventure, so he talked me into going to Santa Fe. The way we figured it, Santa Fe would soon be part of an independent Mexico, when they are successful in their war of independence against Spain. The war between the two started in 1810 and now in 1820 it seemed like everything we heard favored Mexico winning the war.

Santa Fe had been established in 1610 as a Spanish Colony, so until now all of the merchants from outside their own country had come from Spain. When Mexico became an independent country, Santa Fe would be needing lots of new trading partners. Many of those partners would still come from within Mexico, but we were hoping that many would also come from the United States. Troy and I wanted to be part of the first group of traders that came to Santa Fe from the nearby states of the U.S.

Troy gave me enough trade goods (watches, knives, hand tools and a few weapons) to put a light load on two good pack horses. He also gave me money to be able to travel and live for as much as a year. Troy had done well in New Orleans to be able to bankroll me the way he did. But he wanted to do better and frankly I wanted him to do better also. He was a good man and would be an outstanding leader for whatever community he lived and traded in. That's pretty much the way the Rampys have done it from the beginning. They worked hard and always did their best.

Our father told us that in every group of people, someone needed to step forward and provide leadership. He thought we Rampys should be the ones to take the lead, if nobody else was volunteering. That wasn't because we were better than everyone else, but because we were always ready to work.

The journey had been interesting so far. After leaving New Orleans, I took a ferry across the Mississippi with Morgan and the two pack horses.

Morgan was a large athletic bay that loved to run. He was probably a hand taller than most other horses I had seen. One of the pack horses was a roan that I called Roan. The other was a buckskin that I called Buck. Yes, of course, imagination was not my long suit. They were all good horses and did what I needed them to do.

The Mississippi was inspirational. It was huge and powerful. And it was certainly not a river that you could walk your horses across. The countryside was wide open and swampy on both sides of the river. The river itself when I first saw it was almost a mile wide. I had never seen so much water in my life.

I rode west until I got to the Atchafalaya River. Then I rode along the Atchafalaya to where the Red River flowed into it. I followed the Red River through the northwest part of Louisiana and eventually into land now being claimed by Spain. My plan was to avoid both Indians and Spanish soldiers as much as possible.

There wasn't much in the way of settlements in the entire area I would travel, especially once I got into Spanish territory. I did pass west of Baton Rouge, the capital city of Louisiana. It was on the Mississippi about a half day's ride east of the Atchafalaya.

It would have been interesting to visit. Having been established in around 1700, it was a good size town now. But I decided there would be another time to explore Baton Rouge. For now, I had a long way to go and didn't want to waste any time.

The northwest part of Louisiana was heavily covered with trees, so I was obscured most of the time if anybody was looking for me. But anybody looking for me was easily obscured also.

It was pleasant country, except for the heat and humidity. The water kept the humidity high, and the trees kept any breezes to a minimum. Consequently, with the humidity, it felt even hotter than it was. I felt like I was melting most of the time. Water just poured off of me and the horses as well.

The humidity made me concerned about my weapons rusting, so I cleaned them as often as I could and kept them oiled. I carried two Hawken rifles and two Henry 1813 pistols. They were good weapons and I tried to take care of them. Since they were all breach-loaded weapons, I kept all the necessary equipment for care and loading close at hand. My dad always said, "If you take care of your weapons, they will take care of you". Out here by myself, those were important words to live by.

I was in Spanish territory by the time the first Indians came across my path. It wouldn't be the last. I had been warned that Indians liked to trade sometimes, but they could also be fairly unsociable if you were in their territory uninvited. Unfortunately, my whole trip to Santa Fe would fit into the category of uninvited. And since I was traveling by myself, avoiding trouble would be the best plan.

I was hoping to get across Indian land as quickly and easily as possible. I planned to ride rather slowly in order to kick up as little dust as possible. Hopefully, I could keep away from areas where one would have expected Indians and other people to be, especially near water. I would camp carefully at night and leave as little in the way of tracks as possible.

This night, Morgan was restless after dark, but he finally got still, and I went to sleep. I slept lightly and was awake before dawn. I hesitated but finally made a small fire with twigs and some fluff from the cottonwood trees that sheltered me for the night. I made myself a chicory coffee and then smothered the fire with dirt. My brother had given me a bag of the coffee, from his store, before I left New Orleans on this adventure to the west. He swore it was better than regular coffee. He said it had less bite and I had to agree with him. I was hoping it would last until Santa Fe, because there wouldn't be any stores between here and there. The odds of it lasting to Santa Fe would be mighty slim, so I would try to drink it slowly.

The morning was beautiful with just a slight breeze playing through the cottonwood leaves. A couple of robins chattered at each other from a nearby rocky ledge. Because of the spring and the wet ground around it, there was a grouping of cattails. I pulled up some of the young shoots, peeled them and ate them raw. It wasn't half bad for breakfast. I pulled up a few more and took them with me for later. My mother back home in Alabama would have been proud of me for eating my vegetables, even at the age of twenty-eight.

I saddled Morgan and headed south, away from the river. Even though the camp had been a good walk away from the river, it was still closer than I liked to stay. My preference was about a half mile. This distance should keep people following the river from stumbling into our camp.

I had only gone a few hundred yards before I saw animal tracks in soft soil. They were huge and had to be from a mountain lion. The question from yesterday's carcass was answered. I was glad he was full of deer meat and hadn't needed to do any more hunting last night. I traveled farther south and then turned to the west.

Several times over the next ten days I was able to safely pass by Indian camps. How I was capable of seeing them before they saw me was surprising. I am certainly no scout and have no special skills in that regard. Although I do keep a small telescope in my saddlebags and use it as often as it seems appropriate.

I also grew up in the woods of eastern Alabama hunting for food. That's where the Rampy clan had settled after our ancestors immigrated from Germany in the late 1700's. Our name was originally Rempe but was changed to Rampy for some reason by my grandfather when he got to the United States.

There are four of us boys. Troy is the oldest, then Aubrey, Donald and finally me. I am William L. Rampy and usually go by Bill. We also have four sisters. They are Jo Beth, Onita, Willa and Janette. The girls are back home in Alabama with Ma and Pa.

Our family spoke several languages. Pa spoke German as well as English and Spanish. Ma was from Spain, so she spoke Spanish, French, and English. We kids spoke some of everything.

Ma and Pa were full of wisdom and taught us all to work hard and do what we said we would do. We tried to live by that pattern.

Aubrey and Donald are near home farming and raising livestock. They are both tall muscular guys about 6 feet 2 inches tall and both weigh about 220 pounds. Troy and I are both a little shorter than them at 6 feet 1 inch. I weigh about 190 pounds and Troy weighs a little over 200 pounds. All four of us have dark hair, and while I don't want to say we are handsome, our looks probably would not scare any women too badly.

Troy and I are the wanderers. Troy tried his hand at sailing, working on ships up and down the coast. He went from Alabama to New Orleans and then back up the coast and around Florida to as far north as New England. He almost got in trouble in Wilmington, North Carolina with a gun, so finally thought he had better try something new. That is when he set sail for New Orleans. He seems to have found his calling there and now owns a large store furnishing dry goods to those in New Orleans and to settlers headed west for their fortunes.

Troy had always been fascinated by guns. He liked them all, long or short. And he seems to have passed that liking on to me and our other brothers. For whatever reason, I'll never know, we were all pretty good with anything requiring you to pull a trigger. We all had the coordination and vision to use both rifles and pistols well. No rabbit or squirrel was safe when a Rampy was around. Troy never missed and the rest of us seldom did.

Those skills became necessary once I got into the Indian territory of the Red River valley. My intention had been to be careful enough to escape the view of the local inhabitants. That didn't work well at first. It didn't take me long until I blundered into a small hunting party of Wichita Indians. They saw me before I saw them and set up an ambush for me and my horses. As we approached a small grove of trees where I was thinking I might spend the night, the rear pack horse, Buck, fell back on its lead rope. An arrow had come from the small mound on our right. It had hit solidly in Buck's chest and would be a fatal blow. The rope broke, releasing me to head forward, and I did as fast as I could.

The Indians were over the mound and after me as soon as they got on their ponies. Morgan and the other pack horse, Roan, were relatively fresh because it was early in the day. At first it didn't seem like I was going to outrun the ponies, but slowly the tide turned, and I did get some space between me and them.

As I went over a small rise, I stopped the horses quickly and dropped off Morgan with my favorite Hawken rifle. I thought it was time for a little gamble. I steadied myself against a tree and took a shot at the first pony over the rise and hit it in the front of its chest. The ball must have hit the heart because it dropped like a stone. The party hesitated just long enough for me to have another ball ready. I hit the rider on the second pony. After that, they all turned around to head the other way.

Roan had also been hit by an arrow and lost so much blood that he would only stay with me until sunset. In the morning I loaded what I could from Roan's load onto Morgan. I didn't load much in case we got into another race. I had intended on selling the trade goods I brought with me once I got to Santa Fe. Now it looked like I was just going to be able to learn what I could about Santa Fe and make a few friends. I was certainly going to have to be careful to make it there at all.

2 | THREE WEEKS OUT

It was now ten days past the first chase where my pack horses, Roan and Buck, and my trade goods were lost. Being only a few days past our second chase, my heart was still beating too fast. I was determined to keep heading west. Up until now I had been on the south side of the Red River and keeping away from most Indian tribes and any Spanish soldiers, for that matter.

I had seen several different groups of Indians from a distance. Some were tribes with camps set up and others had been hunting parties away from their camps temporarily. The Spanish soldiers had not existed in this part of the country. At least I hadn't seen any. The war for Mexican Independence seemed to be taking place at locations farther south.

The countryside had changed a great deal in the past three weeks. When I left New Orleans, the ground had been swampy and filled with trees, creeks, and ponds. It was beautiful, but the lack of wind and the added humidity made the heat almost unbearable. The creeks and ponds made it difficult at times to stay on course. There was a large variety of trees, but the bald cypress was the most common in the swampiest areas. In most places it was covered with Spanish moss. The combination of the bald cypress and the Spanish moss gave an unearthly feeling to the land as I rode through it. It seemed like places I imagined when my dad told us stories as little kids.

As my route took me farther into the northwest corner of Louisiana, my path was more often on solid ground. And there were more open areas along the river, at least part of the time. The countryside was almost all forest, particularly if you got away from the river.

Forested land was still common until I got a week into the land claimed by Spain. Then eventually the land became more prairie than forest. Then finally there were practically no trees at all. At that time, tall grasses became the main plants, with trees only being along the river and in valleys where there was a source of water. Finally, the grass seemed to get shorter and shorter. It was obvious that it was not just growing shorter because of lack of moisture; but was actually a different type of grass.

My journey had been tiring, but extremely interesting. Before now I was familiar with the plants that grew in Eastern Alabama. I also knew some of the plants along the coast, but I had never been through this type of country, and it was entirely new to me.

One afternoon I had a chance meeting with a Mexican traveler when we both stopped at the same water hole for a drink. He was a ruggedly handsome Mexican gentleman about six feet tall. He was dressed for traveling and had a tall horse with a beautiful saddle. He looked prosperous.

At first glance we were a little wary of each other, but we finally greeted each other. I said, "Buenos Dias. Mi nombre es Bill. Voy a Santa Fe'"

He said, "Hola Bill. Mi nombre es Sebastian. Me voy a El Paso del Norte. Tienes familia en Santa Fe?"

I told him that I didn't have family in Santa Fe but was going there on business. He said he lived in El Paso but had been back east visiting his brother who had moved to America.

Sebastian and I had a conversation as we rested. He was a rancher in an area just north of El Paso. He was born and raised in that area. He and his wife, Deloris, had four children. I told him about my family and my plans to spend the winter in Santa Fe and then return to New Orleans.

As we were both leaving to resume our journeys, Sebastian told me that the river would have several branches as I continued west. The first branch, which he called the Salt Fork, went farther north. Then later another couple of branches would take off to the northwest. He said the Red River would finally become what he called the Prairie Dog Fork of the Red River. He suggested I continue on to the west on that fork. It would take me through a long, beautiful canyon, but would keep me closer to water and wildlife for food. As I was getting low on food, that sounded like the best option. There were some Indians, so I would need to stay watchful he warned.

Another day and a half brought me to what Sebastian called the North Fork of the Red River. By evening of the next day, we got to the Salt Fork. Sebastian had told me that there was good cattle country up that way. He said there were miles and miles of rolling hills with good grass and plenty of water. I made a mental note of that in case I was looking for a place to ranch someday. That was not my interest now, so I headed on west as the Salt Fork took off toward the northwest. I had been staying a bit too close to the river channel, so I wouldn't miss the Salt Fork when it came along. It was time now to get back into the low hills on the south side of the river.

Having left on this adventure from New Orleans in the midsummer, I had made good time by my calculations. Now it was getting into late summer. There was still a long way to go, so slowing down was not a good idea. I needed to be careful about how hard I pushed Morgan.

I had been caring for Morgan as well as I knew how. He seemed to be strong and healthy. I thanked God for that. I certainly wouldn't know what to do if I lost him.

Up to now most of the Indians I had run across were on the north side of the Red. There seemed to be more streams running into the Red from that direction and the country was a little greener. I was happy to stay on the south side of the river and usually counted on springs for water.

If water wasn't available, then I would head up to the river in the dark of the night and get water. This plan worked well until I came over a series of hills one afternoon and saw the biggest Indian camp I had ever seen. And it was right in my path, probably no more than two miles away. It was really lucky I hadn't run into any of their scouts.

I backed down off the high ground easily trying not to stir up any dust or make any quick motions. Then I turned around and headed east back to lower ground. When I found a good river crossing, I would cross and see what the north side of the river looked like.

Being a bit shook up at this point over almost stumbling into the biggest trouble ever, I was moving cautiously. Other people who had spent time in the west said that Indians could be really friendly once you got to know them. I was willing to try that someday; but today wasn't the day.

Riding back down the gully I had come up, I found a secluded grove of trees that would make a good camp. I got the saddle off Morgan and brushed him down good and gave him some water. There was enough water in a leather pouch I always carried for both Morgan and me to have enough to drink. We would drink again when we got to the river, but I wanted to rest now.

Before the sky got completely dark, I eased out to an area above the river to look for a crossing. Being later in the year, the water was running relatively low. Making a night crossing when the river was running deeper would have been too dangerous. I spotted a place back down the river where the river ran over a bed of gravel. Then I went back up to our camp site and got some rest.

I woke up from a restless sleep when the chill of the night had covered the afternoon's heat. I got Morgan saddled and loaded with what supplies we still had, and we took off toward the river. I didn't get in the saddle thinking it might be best for me to lead the way in the dark. A crescent moon was up, but it was low in the sky and there were clouds enough to make it pretty dark. As we got close to the river I saddled up and rode on till I found the gravel bed. I had crossed many a stream and small rivers on Morgan. We had always gotten along well, until this night.

The water was deeper than I expected and running some-what faster. Thinking this was our best option I continued across the gravel bed. It was smooth and solid, making it easy for us to cross at first. But suddenly, when we were nearing the north bank, the gravel disappeared, and we dropped into a deep pocket. Morgan was swimming, which unnerved me. I was trying to decide what to do, but there was nothing I could do until we got closer to the bank. My biggest concern was that the saddle might come loose and dump me and the gear off. It could also get tangled under Morgan, making it impossible for him to swim. My only thought was to stay upright and balanced in the saddle.

After about fifty yards the water started to get shallower again. Morgan finally got a foothold and was able to get to the north bank. It had been way too dark for a crossing, but we made it safely. Hopefully we hadn't been seen by anyone either back on the south bank or on the north bank to which we had just come.

I rode up the far bank into a clearing and dropped down

from Morgan's back. His saddle needed to stay on until we were able to investigate our situation here on the north side of the river. We were both shaking. After a good brushing, Morgan relaxed, and we rode on. I needed to get a little distance from the river to make sure this area was safe.

A shallow valley took us back up toward the hills where I found a camp site. I found some good grass and water for Morgan and picketed him securely by a small pond, for the short night we had left.

I woke later that morning to the chatter of robins and several other birds, the pungent aroma of sage and the smell of good leather from my saddle under my head. It was going to be a good day. I had a quick breakfast of beef jerky and some remaining crumbs of dry bread. Then I got Morgan loaded with our gear and I headed farther north away from the river. After we were well out of sight of anybody near the river, I headed west.

There was no further sign of Indians that day or the next. On the third day there was some dust down on the other side of the river. It appeared to be a small Comanche hunting party. I went farther to the north to stay out of sight.

That afternoon I had to cross a large creek that came into the river from the north. If I had gotten Sebastian's directions right, this was probably the last large creek before the river would continue on as the Prairie Dog fork.

It took another day of cautious riding to get to the canyon that the Prairie Dog fork of the Red River would pass through. The scenery began to change rapidly at that point.

Frankly, it had been a pretty scenic trip with a large variety of changes along the way. From New Orleans along the Atcha-falaya and to the Red River, the country had started out swampy with many streams to cross. As I went farther up the Atchafalaya, the countryside had become more and more wooded. There was an enormous variety of trees after I got out of the swampy areas, where the bald cypress was so common. I saw oaks, hickory, ash, maple, and too many pines and other trees to name.

The Red River was also wooded for a time. It stayed that way for my first week, but had gradually become less and less wooded. Eventually the landscape became prairie. There was tall grass for a while and later the grass became mainly short grass. The countryside had generally been just hilly enough that it provided me cover to stay hidden from anyone that might want to do me harm.

The rugged and colorful Prairie Dog Fork of the Red River provided the best scenery yet. At first, there were many mesquite and salt cedar as the river came down through a continuously growing canyon. Then cottonwoods and poplars got to be more common along with the mesquites and salt cedars.

The canyon walls started to get steeper and steeper. I was beginning to get fearful about whether or not I could get out of the canyon on the other end. Of course, my biggest concern was if we might run into any more Indians. If we did, there would be no way to outrun them. I would have to stand and fight, if fighting was their intent.

The first night in the canyon I watered Morgan down at the river. Then I made camp up a draw about a quarter mile. It was a beautiful place to camp. I sat on a boulder and watched the river. I saw many deer, raccoons, coyotes and skunks, but no sign of Indians. The air was cool and the birds were making themselves at home. There were more doves, meadow larks, robins, and sparrows than I could count. The soil was unusually red throughout most of the canyon. The river had been getting smaller as we went west, but here in the canyon, it was almost a stream or creek. There was still water but not a lot of it. I thought back to our night crossing, when Morgan was swimming in water for fifty yards or so, after we had already crossed most of the river. The stream here was down to no more than fifteen to twenty feet across at the most.

Not long after I started the next morning, I saw the most

overwhelming scenery yet. The walls of the canyon rose right to the sky. They had spectacular colors from white and cream to deep reds and purples. This canyon, like most canyons, had been formed by erosion from the water of the river, but how it had come to look like this, was pretty much a miracle. The canyon was one amazing place. It was filled not only with beautiful colored walls and a wide variety of plants, but with wildlife you can't imagine. It even had rock towers and sheer cliffs.

As the canyon walls got higher and steeper, I had been concerned that this might be a box canyon leaving me no way to get out at the end. As luck was with me, I was able to get out of the canyon. I just followed the Prairie Dog fork until it became a smaller and smaller stream and eventually nothing. This was just about the time I had completed a gradual; but rugged climb out of the canyon.

From here on I would have no water course to follow. I was out on the high prairie and knew basically that I needed to go west to get to Santa Fe. I wasn't sure how much farther I needed to go but was hoping that Morgan and I could get there before the weather turned cold. It was already late summer, so I might not have much time left. Santa Fe was at a higher elevation than here on the prairie and would get cold quicker. I had been traveling slowly and carefully to avoid Indians and Spanish soldiers, but now I was thinking that I should have traveled faster.

Just before I had left the Prairie Dog Fork of the Red River completely, I managed to kill a small deer and smoked some of the meat to carry with me. I also dug some Jerusalem Artichokes to take along. I would either eat them raw or roast them in some coals in a campfire. There were also some late season mushrooms that I was familiar with from back home in Alabama. Usually I don't eat mushrooms, but I recognized these and was certain they were not poisonous. I filled my water bags with every drop of water they would hold and started west.

Traveling across this short grass prairie was not exactly scenic; but you could make good time. After a few days of leaving water behind, I was growing concerned about water. I didn't need too much water; but Morgan had to have a good bit to keep going. As luck would have it (and we Rampy's were usually luckier than most), I found a draw where there was an oasis of sorts. Well, it was a sand oasis. It was a sandy spot with a bit of salt cedar and some cottonwoods. I found a likely spot and got busy with a small shovel I always carried. After digging about two and a half feet, I hit wet soil and then water. I cleared out the hole deep enough that I could fill my water bags after the sand settled out of the water. Then Morgan got to have a good long drink.

It was early evening, so Morgan was picketed with a light-weight rope tied to a stake pushed deep into the ground. This was to keep him from walking off. Then I settled in for the night.

It was quiet out on the prairie under this calm cloudless sky. Laying down on my bed roll as soon as it got dark, the stars were amazing. I had never experienced a night with so many stars. They seemed to light up the sky. I fell asleep looking at the Milky Way.

Morgan was watered and saddled early the next morning and I was on my way west. From looking at the stars the night before I was pretty sure we were on the right course. Between the sun's course during the day and especially the stars at night, direction was not usually a problem for me. Oh, I would admit I had gotten turned around a time or two on cloudy days. But today the sun was up on a beautiful cloudless day and Morgan and I were headed toward Santa Fe.

Water was not as hard to find as I thought it might be, as long as you were willing to dig for it. As we proceeded west there was a constant series of little water courses that crossed our path. Of course, they were dry most of the time; but if you knew where to look and didn't mind digging, the water was there.

The farther west I rode the higher the elevation got, or that was the way it seemed. The air was getting thinner, and my breathing was getting more difficult. I was used to sea level, and this was certainly not sea level.

At another sand oasis one afternoon I was startled to run into a group of people. They were as startled as I was, and the two men reached for their weapons. They appeared to be Mexican, so I hollered, "Hola, estoy solo. Soy un viajero como ustedes. Mi nombre es Bill Rampy."

The older of the two men growled in English. "Well, Bill Rampy, what are you doing out here by yourself? Didn't you know that it could be dangerous in this country?" He laughed a loud rowdy laugh. Then he and the younger man lowered their weapons. He said, "Come have some water from this refreshing spring."

I said, "Thank you, I believe I will."

"My name is Ricardo Poso and this is my son Rodrigo. My wife Imelda and other son Francis are over there. Where are you from, Bill? I'm sure it is not anywhere close to here."

I said, "I am from the United States state of Alabama. I am going to Santa Fe to investigate selling dry goods to merchants there in the coming years. I can't help but think that Santa Fe will be looking for more suppliers when Mexico wins their war of independence and Spanish suppliers become less common."

"Interesting idea, Bill," said Ricardo. "You'll have to talk to a cousin of mine in Santa Fe. Carlos Poso has a store with all kinds of merchandise. I'm sure that he has some of the same things you are wanting to sell. I do know that much of what he sells, he gets from places many miles away in central and southern Mexico. Please look him up when you get there and tell him you met me on the trail, and I asked you to say hi."

"Ricardo, I will certainly do that. Are you from Santa Fe?"

"Yes, that is where we live," Ricardo said. "But I have a sick brother, Franco, who has a rancho south of here. He is unable to work, so we are going to spend the winter with him to help on the rancho. We will be back in the spring, when things warm up and there is no chance of snow. I have an orchard and a small rancho in the area around Santa Fe, but I leased it out to a neighbor for a while so that I could spend time with my brother."

Ricardo told me how to get to Santa Fe. He said I should soon be crossing the Pecos River and then would get to the Sangre de Cristo Mountains. I told them I would look them up when they got back in the spring as I was intending to spend the winter in Santa Fe. I told them it was wonderful to meet them and I looked forward to seeing them again in the spring. They all said they looked forward to seeing me again too.

I saddled up and rode west toward the Pecos River and from there on to Santa Fe. Much of the land was rougher than I expected. I needed to make time and could have if I hadn't spent part of each day working to find water. The land got even dryer as I got closer to the Pecos. The Posos had warned me that the land was dry. Water could always be found by watching the wildlife and birds. There were creek beds fairly often as I proceeded west. While water was not often on the surface, it could usually be found by digging, as I had many times before. The land was dry with only short grasses and sage brush. Occasionally there was salt cedar and cottonwoods, but these were only in areas where water sometimes accumulated.

The Posos had told me to expect to see Spanish soldiers after I crossed the Pecos. I had technically been in Spanish Territory most of the time since a week or so after leaving New Orleans but had never seen any soldiers and only a few Spanish or Mexican citizens. Most of the people I met had been travelers like me. The most common people I did see occasionally and really didn't want to disturb were Indians. This was their territory and I felt like I was trespassing. There were many different tribes from Caddo, Wichita, Tonkawa, Tawankoni and Waco in the east, to Comanche, Kiowa and Kiowa Apache in the west.

There were also different tribes to the north and south.

I had been vigilant and careful. Things had gone well so far, except for my two skirmishes several weeks earlier. As I got farther west there seemed to be less of an Indian presence. Maybe it was because of the lack of water or maybe the Spanish soldiers that the Posos had mentioned.

As I got closer to the Pecos, the ground got sandier and hillier. There were huge mounds of sand that I really enjoyed riding through. You could get on top of the tall mounds to see the countryside ahead yet be secluded for long distances between the hills. I began to see more birds as I got closer to the river. I had left the Posos about two days earlier, so I was expecting to see the river soon. The nights were starting to get a little cool and I sure wanted to get on to Santa Fe as soon as I could. The next afternoon I got to the bank of the Pecos River. I was tempted to camp right there for the night and cross the river in the morning, but something told me to push on across while Morgan was warm. I'm glad we did.

The crossing was better than I expected. It might have been rough if Morgan and I had both been stiff from a cool night. I was lucky on two counts. First, it was late in the season and the water flow was low. And second, I got to the river where the bed was wide, flat, and shallow. I must have been lucky enough to hit the best crossing in the area.

There was a sheltered camping spot about a mile down the trail that headed directly to Santa Fe. It appeared that many people must have come this way before. I had been concerned about having to find my own way to Santa Fe even though the Posos had done their best to describe the trail to me. We were paralleling the Pecos a lot of the way to Santa Fe. I wanted to cross at this point, on relatively flat ground, so we wouldn't need to do it after we got into the Sangre de Cristo Mountains.

That night I made a small campfire for some coffee and roasted Jerusalem Artichokes. They were tubers from a plant that was much like a common sunflower when it was still blooming. These had stopped blooming for this season. And I found some wild greens in the water along the edge of a stream feeding into the river. I was familiar with them. I rinsed them off and ate them without need of any cooking. They had a peppery taste.

When I was finished eating, I covered the coals with just enough dirt that I could still feel the heat. I bedded down close to the warm dirt and went to sleep.

I woke up refreshed in the morning. I was surprised that the mound of dirt was actually still a little warm. Gently scraping the dirt off the old coals, I found some live embers. With some dried leaves, twigs, and shredded cottonwood bark, I got the fire started again and made another cup of coffee. I enjoyed the coffee, then got Morgan saddled up, and got back on the trail.

The first day we went through more sand hills, but after that, things were starting to change. The ground got rougher and brushier. There were still mesquite and sage; but now there was pinyon pine. I had never seen them before, but the Posos had described them to me.

I gathered some of the cones thinking I would try to get to the seeds later. Supposedly, if you burn the cones, it was much easier to extract the seeds. The Posos had shared some of their seeds with me and they were worth the effort it took to extract them from the cones.

The trail was getting steeper and the leaves on some of the trees were changing colors. They were the most beautiful yellow I had ever seen.

On the afternoon of the second day across the Pecos, I heard noise coming from up ahead on the trail. As I topped a small hill, I saw six or seven Spanish soldiers coming my way up the trail. They saw me when I saw them. I couldn't avoid them. I rode on toward them and was flagged over by a soldier that was third in line and appeared to be an officer and the senior person. He spoke loudly and demanded, "Que haces aqui y como te llamas?"

I answered calmly, "Me voy a Santa Fe. Me llamo Bill Rampy." And then I added, "Voy alli por negocios". When I explained to the officer, I was going to Santa Fe for business, he was satisfied with my explanation. He said I could go, but then as an afterthought, he enquired what type of business I was in. I told him I was a trader in dry goods, and, unfortunately, I had lost my pack horses and the merchandise they carried. I told him I intended to get to know some of the local traders and spend the winter in Santa Fe.

He said I was free to go. He also added that they were patrolling along the Pecos and would be back in Santa Fe soon.

In front of me were the formidable Sangre de Cristo Mountains. I was getting more concerned about getting to Santa Fe before the first snow. In fact, I could already see some snow on the peaks of the mountains. I was going straight for Glorieta Pass and just hoped I could get over it without getting caught in bad weather. That was looking less likely by the day.

The Pecos had been heading more northerly than the trail and we had completely lost it at this point. I was tempted to keep moving forward and not stop. However, Morgan had been working hard for the last two days as we had begun to climb into the mountains, so I decided to stop for the night to give him a rest. I found a comfortable spot off the trail and made camp. There was a patch of grass where Morgan could be picketed. After taking off his saddle and brushing him, I spread a blanket over him for the night.

It was really cold that night and began to snow just before dawn with big heavy flakes. I got up quick and saddled Morgan. We were on the trail by first light. The snow was coming down heavy and building up on the trail. It was heavier than I imagined it might be. We trudged on up the mountain until mid-afternoon with only a few short stops. I was beginning to get more concerned, when suddenly at the top of a small hill, I realized we had gotten to the pass. From here on to Santa Fe it might be rugged, but nothing worse than we had already been through. And, as fate would have it, the snow was tapering off and finally stopped about the time we made camp for the night.

I had found a protected place to camp in a group of trees. The snow hadn't gotten under the dense canopy made by the trees, so it was still clear. I unsaddled Morgan and put the blanket back over him for protection again. I got a small fire started for some coffee and warmth.

I was encouraged by the day. We had gotten over the pass and should be able to get to Santa Fe in a few days, if everything continued to go well.

In the morning, as usual, I brushed the dirt off the coals of last night's fire and found to my pleasure some live coals and the three pinyon pinecones I had put on top of the coals to roast. I started the fire and then tried breaking the cones apart to get the seeds out. It worked well and I soon had a little pile of the seeds. I broke the hard shell of the seeds with my teeth and ate the seeds one by one. They were rich and had a meaty flavor. The seeds made a good breakfast along with my coffee.

3 | SANTA FE

By the afternoon of the next day, I made it to the outskirts of Santa Fe. Numerous small adobe houses were scattered along the road. Most of them had at least one dog barking a "greeting". Everyone that I saw was friendly, yelling, "Hola senor" as I rode by. I yelled "Hola" back to them.

The trail was obviously used a lot and had become more of a road than a trail. However, the road had a few twists and turns as it avoided rock outcroppings and large trees. This was a forested area. The evergreen trees were mostly pines and cedars, but there were some broadleaf trees with bright yellow leaves. I wasn't familiar with them until I started seeing them a few days ago, but they certainly added to the beauty of the area. I was pretty sure I was going to like spending time in Santa Fe.

After some time, the small houses gave way to commercial enterprises. I thought about stopping, but I wanted to get to the center of town first. The Posos told me there was a large square with the Governor's Palace right in the center of town. To the east and north a block or so from the square was a beautiful cathedral. I was coming into town from the south and could make out the cathedral from a distance. After more than two months I had finally made it to Santa Fe. Next time it should be a much quicker trip, but this time I tried to be as cautious as I could since I was alone.

My intentions, at this point, were to learn as much as I could about trade coming into and going out from Santa Fe. Before I lost my other two horses and the merchandise they carried, I had intended to make contact with the area merchants and sell what I had brought with me. I also wanted to find out what they needed for their stores and where they usually got it. Then I planned to go back to New Orleans to work with Troy and open a trading business with these local merchants, if that seemed like it would be profitable. Now, I intended to spend the winter in Santa Fe and learn what I could about the needs of the people and merchants of this area.

The road led me right to the square. It was impressive, with the Governor's Palace on the west side of the square and a variety of businesses around the other three sides. All the businesses were made of adobe. Some were larger than others, but the Governor's Palace was by far the largest and most ornate. It had a covered porch running the full length of the building. It was made of large round beams that appeared to have been made of an entire medium size tree. You could tell that the roof and walls of the palace were made of similar beams.

Directly across the square from the Governor's Palace was a hotel. That sounded like a good place to start my time in Santa Fe. The front door was open, so I walked in. A gentleman who was probably in his mid-forties greeted me from behind a small white counter. He said, "Bienvenido Senor. ¿Puedo ayudarlo?"

"Si, quisiera una habitacion para pasar la noche y algo de comida," I responded.

Changing to English he said, "We have both, sir. I'll talk to my wife in the back. What would you like?"

"Enchiladas with beef or lamb would be good. But what

does your wife prefer to cook?" I added as an afterthought. "I've been riding for several months and just about anything would be wonderful."

His wife's food was wonderful. She cooked beans like I had never eaten before. They were medium brown with a soft and creamy texture. She also cooked a medium size steak with tortillas on the side. In addition, there were some roasted root vegetables that she had grown in her own garden. The meal was as good as I had ever had.

After supper Mr. Espinosa took me to my room and told me he would heat some water for a bath. I took Morgan out back to a little stable owned by the hotel. I brushed him down vigorously and gave him some water and hay. Then I went back in the hotel and took my bath in a private room with a metal tub. After the bath I went back to my room and settled in for the night. The bed had a straw tick mattress and a small pillow. I went to sleep the minute my head hit the pillow. It was the first bed I had slept on since I left New Orleans.

I woke in the morning to a soft knock on the door. Mr. Espinosa said that his wife was cooking breakfast. I got up quick. I wasn't about to miss her breakfast.

"Good morning, sir. What would you like for breakfast?" asked Mrs. Espinosa.

"What have you got?" I asked.

She told me what she had and I settled on one egg, two tortillas and some fried cornmeal mush with syrup. There was also coffee. It was as good as supper the night before. This was truly a place to remember.

After breakfast, I walked around town for most of the morning and then went up on the hotel porch. I sat there quite a while enjoying the day. The sun was shining, but it felt crisp. It would have felt cold if there had been any breeze. I could smell wood smoke from all over town. There were birds flying here and there, mainly chickadees, goldfinches, robins and crows. I didn't see any other larger birds. I assumed they had already gone south to a warmer climate.

Mr. Espinosa came out onto the porch and said, "How did you sleep last night?"

I turned his way and said, "Excellent. Thank you. I usually sleep fairly well; but there is no comparing a patch of hard ground to a real mattress."

"Yes, I know that is true. I have also spent my time on the trail. Is Santa Fe your destination or are you going farther?"

"I hope to spend the winter here and go back to New Orleans in the spring. My brother and I trade in dry goods. I came this way with a load of goods for sale but lost them on the way. My brother had an old friend up this way who also did a bit of trading, so I am hoping to find him. His name is Leos. Juan Leos. Have you heard of him?"

Mr. Espinosa leaned back in his chair and gave me a funny look. Then he laughed. "Juan Leos is an extremely good friend of mine. In fact, he is more than a friend. He is my wife's brother. How did your brother say he had met Juan?"

I scratched my head and said, "I'm not sure, but I think it involved sailing and then working in Savannah."

He laughed again and said, "That sounds like Juan. He is the adventurer in his family. He left Santa Fe when he was young and traveled around. He learned some of several languages while he sailed on a couple of ships. He came home to Santa Fe about five years ago. Then he left Santa Fe again and spent a winter trapping up north in the big mountains. He got to know many trappers and decided he would rather sell supplies to them instead of competing with them for pelts. Many of them are extremely good trappers with skills taught by years of experience. Juan felt like he could not compete with them. Now he lives about a day's ride north of here in the direction of Taos. He trades with trappers, Indians, and anybody else who comes along."

"Could you tell me how to get to his place? I would like to meet him and give him a message from my brother," I responded.

He said, "I certainly can. And by the way, my name is Alphonse." Then he stuck out a big hand and shook mine with real enthusiasm. Then he grabbed me and gave me a big hug. I wasn't used to being hugged by anybody except my family, so it shocked me.

I said, "I'm Bill, Alphonse."

Then Alphonse continued, "Bill, why, don't you plan on staying another night with us and I'll take you around to meet a few businesspeople in town this afternoon. You can get a good start in the morning and be to Juan's place by late afternoon. Or, if you're not in a hurry, you could spend several more days here before you head off."

"That would be great. I really would like to see Juan as soon as possible, so I will plan to leave in the morning," I said.

"Sounds like a good idea," Alphonse said. "Let's go back into the dining room and have lunch before we go walking around."

Lunch was light, which was good because I was not used to eating lunch on the trail. It was especially nice to get to know Alphonse and his wife Christine better. They both had spent most of their lives in Santa Fe and known each other since childhood. They had no children, but several nieces and nephews that all lived in the area. Their parents were both born in Spain but met in Mexico after their parents immigrated to Mexico in a large group. They and most of their family spoke both Spanish and French. Some of them spoke a good deal of English.

"Let's go, Bill. I'll introduce you to some people. Some of them are family, but all of them are also good friends," suggested Alphonse.

"I'd love to meet all of your friends and family, Alphonse, or as many as we have time for," I laughed.

We first were off to meet his cousins Manuel and Leon. They were twins and both of them were well over an average man's height and weight. At what I would judge to be six foot five inches or so, they were each bigger than anyone I had ever met. I thought my family was full of big guys, but not like this. They both chose appropriate businesses. Manuel was Santa Fe's only blacksmith and Leon made freight wagons which apparently were selling well.

We stopped by Leon's shop first. It was sort of like a cabinet shop but bigger.

Alphonse saw Leon first and said, "Leon, I want you to meet Bill Rampy. He is a businessman from New Orleans. He came here to spend the winter and learn about the dry goods business in our area. His brother Troy is an old friend of Juan. They used to sail together along the east coast of the United States. He is heading out tomorrow to meet Juan."

Leon said with a laugh, "Bill, you will probably be wanting to buy one of my wagons soon to carry some of your dry goods."

Leon had a jolly personality and never took anything seriously. He had a mustache that seemed to cover half of his face. Drooping down over his mouth, I couldn't help but wonder how he was able to eat with a mustache like that. He was obviously able to manage or he wouldn't have been able to get to what I judged to be over three hundred pounds.

"You're probably right, Leon, but I don't think I'm ready right now," I chuckled. They were sturdy wagons built out of wood just thick enough to hold a load, but not cause weight problems. The axles and wheels were also stoutly built and probably would carry the wagons as far as the owners wanted them to go. The wagons also had stacked carriage springs that should give a smooth ride for the driver and cargo.

I hoped there would come a day when I needed one or maybe more of these wagons, maybe many more. Alphonse and I had a great time looking at Leon's wagons and talking to him about Troy and Juan.

It was a chilly day, so our visit to Manuel's blacksmith shop was just right considering the heat his work created. His work was part horse shoeing and part creating odds and ends that local business people needed for equipment repair. He also made knives and hand tools, amongst other things. Alphonse showed me a knife Manuel had created that had a strong ten-inch drop point blade and an elk horn handle. It was, in my estimation, extremely well done.

Alphonse introduced me. "Manuel, I want you to meet Bill Rampy. He is in the dry goods business in New Orleans and his brother is a close friend of Juan. They did a lot of sailing together."

Manuel came over and stuck out one of the biggest hands I had ever seen. He looked even bigger than Leon. "Hi Bill. It is nice to meet you," he said. "And if your brother is a close friend of Juan that makes you practically family. So, welcome to the family."

Manuel was friendly like Leon but not as exuberant. He shook my hand hard but he didn't hug me. He seemed more focused and easy-going than Leon.

"Thanks, Manuel. From what I have seen of your family, I would be proud to be a member. I have never actually met Juan. I hope he feels the same way when I meet him. I'm planning to go meet him tomorrow."

"Be careful up that way," Manuel warned. "I had a friend that came through that same area just a few days ago and said that he saw three mountain lions and heard growls several more times. You always have to be aware of their presence. He thinks that their numbers were larger than normal. And if they are competing with each other for food, they might be hungrier than normal and more dangerous."

"Thanks for the warning, Manuel," I replied. "I'll be as careful as I can be. Usually my horse, Morgan, can sense them being around and lets me know by his skittishness. As I was following the Red River from Louisiana on my trip here, I saw the evidence of mountain lions several times in one area. Fortunately, though, I didn't hear anything from them for the rest of the trip."

Alphonse and I visited with Manuel for a while about blacksmithing and growing up in Santa Fe. It was obvious from my conversations with Manuel, Leon, and Alphonse that family was important to all of them. I was glad to hear that because I felt the same way about my family back in Alabama and New Orleans.

After our conversation with Manual, we moved on down the street to meet a few more friends. He introduced me to a clothier, a grocer, two attorneys, and the local doctor. All of them had grown up here in Santa Fe and had known Alphonse's family for years.

Alphonse and I eventually headed back to the hotel to have supper and call it a day. I had pretty much a full day riding to get to Juan's place per Alphonse's directions, so that would need to wait until tomorrow.

Christine had a wonderful supper ready for us when we returned. It consisted of refried beans, beef enchiladas, tortillas and chili rellenos. We ate and ate and praised Christine for her cooking. Then we talked for an hour or so. I was beginning to feel like family. I finally started to get tired and went to bed. Morning was going to come way too early.

I was up and out at the corral brushing and saddling Morgan before first light. I talked to Morgan softly to make up for not seeing him much for the past few days. The relationship between a horse and his rider was important and I wanted to keep ours strong. Morgan and I had been together for about a year. I had ridden many horses but never a better one than Morgan. He was two years old when I bought him from a family friend back in Alabama. The friend had broken and trained him. He liked Morgan and wanted to keep him himself, but he had too many horses at that time and needed to sell several. I'm glad I came along at the right time.

About the time Morgan and I were all set, Alphonse called from the back door of the hotel. "Bill, come on in and get some coffee before you leave. I've got a map I want to give you."

"I'll be right there," I called back.

Christine had made not only some coffee, but some cake and bread. She also had a box of food to keep me "full" along the way. I wasn't sure I needed to be "full", but I wasn't going to refuse the hospitality.

Alphonse had some information and a map on where to find Juan's trading post. "Juan lives near the Rio Grande River northwest of here," he said. "I've got you a map here; but it is fairly simple. Just follow the trail that takes off to the northwest from the Santa Fe River. It will meet up with the Rio Grande. Then go north along the Rio Grande a couple hours, until you see some wooded hills to the east of the river. There is a well-worn path leaving the river at that point. It will take you up into the hills. Juan has a trading post that does a lot of business with trappers and other travelers, so it is easy to find."

"Alphonse, you don't know how much I appreciate your and Christine's hospitality," I said. "I have had a great time here in Santa Fe. And it was especially nice for you to introduce me to your family and friends. I hope to spend some time with Juan, if he will have me, and then come back here for a while. There isn't any use trying to make it back across country to New Orleans until spring, so I am planning to spend the winter here and head back when I can."

"You're welcome back any time. We will look forward to seeing you again soon. Tell Juan hello for us and tell him we will see him the next time he heads this way. I assume that will be when he goes to Chihuahua for the winter market."

"I'll tell him, Alphonse. And I'll look forward to seeing you again soon. Thanks for your hospitality and friendship. Oh, and Christine, thank you so much for the wonderful food. Take care." And with that, Morgan and I were off. Both Alphonse and Christine were waving as I rode away.

4 | JUAN LEOS

There was a well-established trail going out of Santa Fe toward the northwest. The trail would meet up with the Rio Grande eventually. I hoped to follow the Rio Grande north toward Taos soon; but I wasn't going that far today. I wanted to get to know Juan first and then I would go to Taos.

The ground through which the trail passed was rough and rocky in places, but most of the time it was smooth riding. This road had been traveled by thousands of trappers and others over the decades. Most of the way was tree lined. Some of it was wide open with nothing to break the wind or stop the sun. Of course, it was coming on winter, so any sun was welcome. There was no snow on the ground and the wind was icy.

An hour up the trail the sun had gotten fairly high and I was going through a dense stand of trees when Morgan got a little skittish. It made me think about the warning Manuel had given us concerning more mountain lions in this area than normal. At least it was bright day light. I kept my eyes open and my mind working as we moved on. The countryside was rough and beautiful. There was prickly pear cactus and lots of pinyon pine, and what my family had called bear grass. I think I heard Alphonse refer to it as yucca. When I would see it as a kid and it was in bloom, I would eat some of the blooms. They tasted good as long as you ate only the petals and none of the interior parts that were especially bitter. To my right were the Sangre de Cristo Mountains. In front of me was the Rio Grande. Across the river I could see another range of mountains.

I stopped for water and a bite of lunch. Christine had packed a couple of tortillas rolled around some roasted lamb. I enjoyed the lunch a great deal, rested a bit and then moved on to the northwest.

Morgan hadn't been skittish for a while, so I was hoping we might be past the mountain lions.

Just a little way up the trail we were going through a brushy area when Morgan stopped dead in his tracks. I was about to draw my pistol when a small doe shot across the trail in front of us not twenty feet away. Following the doe was a mountain lion at full speed. His mind was focused on the doe, so he barely seemed to notice we were there. I was certainly glad that he didn't stop to greet us. He was the biggest one I had ever seen. We had mountain lions in the forests back home in Alabama, but they were nowhere near this big. The size of this lion really shook me. I didn't know what I would do if he was after me.

I hoped the deer would escape. I decided we had better get out of the lion's territory as quickly as we could.

About thirty minutes took me far enough away from the lion that I was breathing somewhat easier. In the distance I would see that I was approaching the village of Pojoaque. The side trail to Juan's should be coming up on the right. After a few minutes I saw it and turned off the trail toward the trading post. The trail started to get steep and went through some pinyon at first and then a patch of larger pine trees. It was beautiful country looking toward the northeast. Something made me turn around to look back the way I had come. I saw a view I will never forget. It looked down across a huge expanse of the Rio Grande River Valley. To the west across the river was a mountain range running parallel to the river and farther south there was another smaller range of mountains. I could certainly see one of the reasons that made Juan want to live here.

Up the trail another half mile was Juan's trading post. It was a well-built log cabin with several outbuildings and a large barn, also made of logs. There was a substantial corral attached to the barn. The buildings all stood at the base of a steep hill. It wasn't actually a cliff, but it would be very difficult to get up and down from the direction of the trading post. The hill was covered with aspen and pine trees. The trading post set on flat ground and was in the middle of an open area of about two acres.

There were two saddled horses hitched in front of the cabin. I got down from Morgan and loosened his saddled a bit and tied him to a post in front of the trading post. Then I went in to meet Juan.

Juan was in a negotiation with two men I took to be trappers. He looked me up and down and then waved me over by the fireplace. I stood there until they were finished talking and left. Juan, or who I assumed was Juan, looked at me and said, "Bienvenidos. Como puedo ayudarte?

I said in English, "If you are Juan Leos, I have come all the way from New Orleans to meet you. My name is Bill Rampy and my brother is Troy Rampy. He says you are a second-rate sailor, but absolutely made of gold otherwise."

It was Juan and he looked almost thunder struck. He came around the counter and gave me the biggest bear hug I had ever had. At about five foot ten inches tall and two hundred pounds, Juan was not nearly as big as his cousins Leon and Manuel, but he was strong as a bear. I thought he was about to break my ribs. He had black hair with an olive brown complexion. He looked to be in his mid-thirties.

"I cannot believe it," he practically yelled. "Speaking of

gold, that is your brother Troy. We were fast friends from the time we met! Troy and I had some great times! We sailed on the "Willa Mae" from Yorktown, Virginia to Boston and then eventually down to Tybee Island near Savannah. We stayed in Savannah for a while and then eventually caught another ship, the Charlotte, that was going to St. Augustine and then on around Florida and along the Gulf Coast. Troy went as far as New Orleans and got off to seek his fortune there. I sailed on another ship, the Veracruz, from there to Matamoros. I bought a horse there and made my way across country back to Santa Fe. It was a long way; but it didn't seem too bad. I was so anxious to get home, that the time flew."

He continued, "Troy and I had a many great adventures together and got into and out of a spot of trouble more times than I would like to admit. He is a great guy! I really thought I would never hear from Troy again. Now to have his brother show up on my doorstep is beyond belief. Welcome, Bill Rampy! I am happy to have you here!"

"Juan, I am happy to be here," I stammered. What else could I do after a reception like this. "Troy told me about some of your adventures together. I am glad you both survived." To this Juan laughed.

Then he asked, "What are you doing here? I never expected a guy from Alabama to make his way to the big mountains."

"Well, Troy sent me in a way," I said. "I had it in my mind to do some exploring in this part of the country and see what kind of adventures I could get into. It's like you two going to the east coast to sail. I wanted to go west to see what I would find. Troy thought I should look for business opportunities. He started a store in New Orleans where he sells about anything the locals or settlers heading west might need. I've worked with him for several years and when I told him my thoughts of exploring in the west, he thought it was a great idea. We knew that Spain and Mexico were in a conflict now and something told us that

Mexico would win. And if and when that happens, we believe there will be large opportunities here for trade. We decided that I should come see what I could learn about the Santa Fe area and its people and any business prospects."

"Bill, I would say you have come to the right place. There are lots of needs here now. When Mexico wins the war, which appears to be likely, there will be more and more business possibilities. Most of my family is in business in one way or the other, so we all look forward to this area growing and the market for goods getting larger."

"It sure does sound like I have come to the right place," I offered. "And met the right family. I hadn't told you yet, but I have already met some of your family."

Juan said, "I assumed somebody I'm related to pointed you this direction. That's one of the advantages of having a large family. Who have you met?"

"I met Alphonse and Christine first at the hotel. Then Alphonse introduced me to Manuel and Leon and several other friends. Once they found out that my brother knew you, they practically adopted me."

That comment made Juan laugh. "Don't you love families? Our family is big and especially close. Well, if they adopted you, I will too. Welcome to the family. Hey, how long are you intending to stay in this area?"

"My idea is to spend the winter and go back to either New Orleans or St. Louis in the spring."

"Great!" Juan said, "And unless you have a better offer, why don't you stay here with me. I've got enough room and enough work. I could feed you and give you a little walking around money too. I would love to have you here and I could use some extra help. And hopefully you might be able to learn a few things about supplying dry goods to this area."

"Juan, it would be good working with you! I can't think of a thing that I would rather do."

Juan and I talked through most of the night about growing up in our respective families. We talked about being kids, going to family gatherings, hunting, fishing, fighting, shooting, reading, and most of all having a burning desire for adventure. The world wasn't known too much to us and our families; but we knew the world was out there and Troy and I wanted to see some of it. Neither of us wanted to see it all, but we did want to see some of it.

For Juan, his sailing experience and going from Santa Fe to the coast and back again was a great adventure. For me, going from Alabama to New Orleans and then on to Santa Fe was the same. We were both going to places that were known and had been explored before, but certainly not by many people and even less by the average person.

Juan had done his exploring and I was doing mine and neither of us intended to stop. Juan was in place for a while and loving his work. He said he was not finished with his journeys. Maybe the west or northwest might be his next big experience. To me getting back to New Orleans or St. Louis was a big enough adventure, for a while.

"Hey, Bill, are you going to wake up today or just stay there on that tick?" Juan yelled across the room the next morning.

I mumbled, "Well, I had been thinking I might just stay here forever. But, if you insist, I will get up."

"If you need an incentive to get up, I do have a little breakfast that might entice you. I made a pot of my special mountain man coffee for you. And I also have some tortillas, beans and back fat."

I could already smell the coffee and back fat, so I was already planning to get up. "Tell me about this mountain man coffee, Juan. I've never had that."

"Oh, sure you have," Juan said. "You just called it something else. When I was trying my hand at trapping up north in the big mountains, I was always afraid I would run out of coffee.

I made it weaker and weaker as the months went by. So, to me mountain man coffee is weak coffee. I hope you can get used to it. If you can't, we can make it stronger. I just got used to making it that way."

I sipped a little of my first cup and said, "You're right. That does taste familiar. I just called mine Red River coffee. Except mine had some chicory in it, so it did taste different than yours. But, I don't think I'll have any trouble getting used to yours.

We sat and had coffee and breakfast and talked some more. Juan told me about meeting Troy and their work together on the ships. And he told me about a few of their adventures in a couple of ports. Obviously, the work was hard; but the adventures made up for it. They got to know a lot of the east coast of the U.S. and met many interesting people. Everywhere they went they met people selling and buying dry goods of all types. That apparently rubbed off on both of them. Juan told me they had discussed both wanting to be dry goods merchants some day when they settled down. Troy talked about going back to Alabama and Juan always wanted to come home to the area around Santa Fe.

"Bill, I thought I would explain my little business to you today," Juan said.

I said, "I would really like to hear all about it." I followed Juan as we looked around the inside of his trading post and he explained his operation.

Juan started, "I basically handle supplies for area people and the trappers that come through. There are some trappers that bring in furs to trade for supplies. Some of them have cash or gold or other odds and ends to trade. I'm actually getting low on some of the supplies I usually keep on hand, so we need to get them restocked."

"How do you get your supplies way out here?" I asked.

"I get some, of course, in Santa Fe," he said. "But once a year I go to Chihuahua to both sell and buy goods at the annual trade fair. I'm glad you're here, Bill. We will have a good time together, both here and on the trip to Chihuahua. Let's go outside and I'll show you around."

Juan's compound had several smaller buildings besides his main building which was also his home. There was a corral where he kept a number of horses and a few teams of mules. There was a barn attached at one end of the corral. It was at the bottom of a large hill and had cottonwood trees on either side. About fifty feet from the corral was another shed that also backed up to the hill. It was probably fifteen feet square. After that was the main building and then another smaller shed. They also backed up to the hill. The hill was steep enough that you could not ride a horse up or down it, and even walking it would be difficult. The hill provided protection for Juan and his operation from at least one direction.

Juan started to explain the layout of the place. "I'll show you the corral first since it is the simplest. I usually keep four or five horses and a team or two of mules on hand. When we go to Chihuahua, we will use most of them. The red dun there is the one I usually ride. I call him Red. He's sure-footed in the hills, can climb in the mountains pretty well, and can run like the wind when he's in the open. The bay and the black against the other fence are both good saddle horses too. The rest of the horses have all been used on wagons a few times each and can hold their own. But they have also been used for riding and carrying loads. The mules are just for wagons, especially when we are hauling heavy loads."

"Do you sell any horses?" I asked Juan.

"Around here, Bill, I will sell anything, if someone with money in hand wants to buy it. Although, I am pretty partial to the red dun and would rather not sell him. Red and I have been together for several years. I generally buy and sell horses, so the numbers change from time to time. The mules, though, are pretty much a permanent fixture here."

I had put Morgan in the corral after leaving him tied up on

the outside until the other horses got used to him. He seemed to get along well with all of them.

Juan showed me the barn. It smelled warm and oddly comfortable. There was gear for the riding horses on the right wall and equipment for the wagons on the left wall. Against the back wall was a large stack of dried native grass hay. Above the hay was an unusual piece of equipment that consisted of a block and tackle and some ropes hanging down behind the pile of hay. It didn't look like it was in use, whatever it was.

Juan noticed me looking at it. "Bill, I can see you're curious about my handy work. Can you figure it out?"

"Not really," I answered. "But it does look like it needs some other piece before it will work. What is it and what do you do with it?"

"It's something that I usually explain to people as being broken," Juan responded. "But it isn't. If you get this hook mechanism from the other side of this beam and hook it to the "broken" piece, then you have a functional lifting device."

He closed the door facing the trail part way. Then he opened the doors toward his cabin. After that he lit a lamp on the wall.

He attached the hook together with the ropes and to another hook that was out of sight behind the pile of grass hay. Then he pulled on one of the ropes and the back of the grass lifted into the air. He tied off the rope to a metal hook on the wall.

Juan said, "Come on. I want to show you something."

Behind the pile of hay was a staircase going down into the ground. The light from the lantern on the wall added to the light coming into the building from the opened large doors, gave enough light to see fairly well in the basement.

As we walked down the stairs, Juan said, "This is one of my secrets. You know a guy out here in the woods needs his secrets. This is where I store rifles and gun powder. I like to keep a lot of it on hand, but don't want it to be known by anybody. I dug this cave below the barn to keep it away from the house. I figure that most people would expect me to keep any weapons in my house. And I do keep some there; but the bulk of them I keep out here. If I'm away for a few days and somebody breaks in, they could get a few rifles and that's all. Well, there are other things in the store that they could get. I just don't want them to get thirty rifles and gun powder." Juan lowered the stack of hay over the staircase and made a few adjustments to make sure the door was well hidden. Then he turned out the lantern and closed the door toward the cabin.

As we walked out of the barn, Juan added, "The horses get spooky if anybody comes into the corral without me. That warns me to be aware of anybody being out this way. That, added to the hidden door and "broken" snatch block should keep out most intruders."

"Well, it sure would keep me out," I offered. "I didn't have any idea what you were doing there. Where do you get the hay anyway? It looks like somebody put in some long hours cutting that."

Juan laughed. He said, "I like to keep some hay around for the horses and am lucky enough to have ground up on top of the hill behind this place that has a good stand of grass. When it is time to harvest, I have a scythe that I use to cut the grass. When it is dry, I have a rake to gather it. I do a little bit at a time. It's not as hard as it sounds. I use Red hooked to a small wagon to haul it into the barn."

"Sounds like real work to me," I said. "I'll probably be gone early enough in the spring that I'll miss the opportunity to help you with that enterprise."

Juan chuckled as we walked over to the shed between the barn and the house. "In this shed is where extra supplies are kept," he said. "I usually keep more staples. There is always salt, coffee, flour, dried beans, and other staples. They are sold to travelers and trappers. Oh, and sometimes to Indians. I'm running pretty low at this point. We'll need to get more soon.

We need to keep whatever we can to supply trappers. Since they go out for months or sometimes a year at a time, they usually have the most need for these items. I also keep other items they may need like rope, string, leather strips, lead, cloth and some basic clothing. Some of those things are kept in the other shed on the far side of the house."

We went back to the house for more coffee and something to eat. I asked Juan, "What brought you to this particular site to build on? Was it the location?"

"It wasn't the location as much as the way the ground lay," he said. "It has a good view out toward the Rio Grande but is sort of secluded. I wanted to be far enough from the regular trail that people weren't stumbling over me. But I also wanted to be close enough to the trail that I could be found by those needing what I have to offer. Most of my business comes to me by word of mouth. And I also wanted some ground that was at the base of a hill. This place seemed perfect to me. The hill faces southwest, so it protects me from a good deal of the cold coming out of the north. I wanted to build my house and outbuildings back against the hill for protection mainly from weather. But I liked the site also because of the security it offers. There are trees between the buildings. That allows me to get from building to building without having to get out in the open."

"Is there a threat from Indians or anyone else?" I asked.

"No, not as much as you would think," Juan answered. "I just like to be cautious. Being out here by yourself can be dangerous, so I just wanted to have the odds in my favor if anything did happen."

Speak of timing. I just stood up as I was finishing my last gulp of coffee when a sight out front made me jump. There were four Apache braves on horseback that had just ridden up in front of the corral. They were looking into the corral. I stammered, "Juan, are those customers of yours or should we get our guns?"

Juan laughed and said, "Yes, they are customers. They come

by from time to time, basically needing supplies; but they are always interested in new ponies. I don't usually have what they are looking for, so they just trade for whatever supplies they need."

Juan moved out onto the porch and raised his hand as sort of a salute. The brave that looked to be the leader did the same. I stayed in the house just to watch the action and keep out of the way. Juan walked over to the leader. The leader motioned toward the corral to start their conversation. Juan shook his head several times. Then they must have gotten down to discussing supplies. After a while Juan came back into the house to get a few things they needed and took them back out. One of the other braves unrolled a bundle and showed Juan a couple of furs. Juan looked at the furs closely and shook his head yes, then took the bundle that was handed to him. That seemed to conclude the trade and the braves turned their ponies and headed back toward the southwest.

Juan came back in the house and said, "They didn't really have much of a shopping list today other than ponies. They still had some furs left over from last season that they used for payment. This will add to the furs I have in the back room. Usually, most trappers get rid of the majority of their furs in the early summer at the Taos Trade Fair. The big fur buyers are there and take most of the best furs; but I get a lot of odds and ends that are left over from trappers coming in later for resupply. I take all that I have to Chihuahua in January."

"How far is Chihuahua?" I asked.

"Oh, it's just about six hundred miles, Bill," Juan answered. "I usually allow thirty days to get down there, especially if I am taking a wagon. This time I plan to take two wagons. We'll need to get there by January 10th, so we should leave in early December. There are several other traders that will want to go with us and they will have wagons too. On a long trip like this it is best to go as a group for companionship and safety. The route is fairly well traveled and generally safe. The only thing we might run into would be young braves trying for some free goods to carry home and a little excitement. But that is pretty uncommon. You should enjoy the trip. I realize long trips are nothing new to you having come all the way from New Orleans."

"Six hundred miles sounds like a pretty good ride, even to me, Juan," I said. "How many times have you made the trip?"

"I've done it more times than I can remember," Juan said. "My family and friends made the trip fairly often when I was growing up. We have family and friends down there too. As an adult I have made the trip six or seven times probably. I think you will enjoy it. And you should enjoy the men who will be going with us. Most of them are my relatives, so I sort of have to like them. But you should like them without even needing to be related," he chuckled. "Hey, we need to go to Santa Fe to pick up some supplies, so let's go tomorrow. I'll introduce you to the men who will be going with us."

"Juan, that sounds great to me," I said. "I just spent a couple of days in Santa Fe before I came up here. It seems like a good town. I would certainly like to get to know it better."

"Oh, you will," he said. "You will."

We spent the rest of the afternoon and evening making sure that Juan's place was good and secure. We bolted the shutters over the windows in the house. After that we made sure the barn and sheds were secure. Then we fed and watered the horses. To-morrow we will head to Santa Fe and spend a few days. On the way we will stop by a friend's cabin to ask him to spend some time at Juan's place to look out for things while we are gone.

5 | TO SANTA FE FOR SUPPLIES

The next morning, we headed to Santa Fe just as the sun was rising. We went east up through the hills. Juan took one packhorse with us to bring back the supplies for the trading post.

Juan knew a quicker way to Santa Fe than I had used. It was beautiful. The smell of the pines was refreshing and the rocky outcroppings here and there in the hills made for dramatic scenery. The trail got enough riders on a regular basis that it was in good shape. There were a few spots where we went up steep areas that would not have been particularly safe, if they were snow covered. I was glad that today it was dry and clear.

We hadn't gone far before we got to Carlos Medina's cabin. Like Juan, Carlos had tried his hand at trapping up in the big mountains; but then he had come home to be closer to friends and family. He still trapped some, mostly in the Sangre de Cristo Mountains. He hunted for meat, raised a garden for vegetables in the summer, and worked for Juan when he was needed. Like Juan, he had lots of family in the area.

Carlos's cabin was smaller than Juan's. It had one main room and two smaller rooms in the rear. There was a rock fireplace toward the back of the main room that opened both to the front and back, so it warmed the entire cabin easily. The hearth was much bigger in the main room than the one in the bedroom. The walls were made of logs chinked together with mud. The logs were not as large as many I had seen on cabins; but this was to keep the logs small enough that one man by himself could work with them. Carlos had done an especially good job. I thought I would like to have a cabin similar to his someday.

Juan and Carlos visited a while and then we were off to Santa Fe. Carlos was working on a shed by his cabin that he hoped to get finished soon. He would make it to Juan's place before sundown and would stay there until we got back.

It was beautiful in the hills as we headed toward Santa Fe. There were good sized mountains to our east; but we skirted them and stayed to the foothills. Several times our horses got a bit skittish, telling us that there were probably mountain lions close by. This didn't bother us much because it was unlikely that they would try to attack two horses and riders together. Still, it was somewhat unnerving to know they were around, particularly now when I knew how large this western variety could be.

We got to Santa Fe about an hour before sundown and went straight to Juan's parent's house on the north side of town. It was a large adobe house that faced south. A sturdy porch covered the entire front of the house. There was a railing across the front made of cedar logs. It also had crossed logs from the railing to the porch. Chimneys were prominent on each end of the house. It had a warm and friendly look.

Juan's parents invited us for supper and to stay with them while we were in town. Fortunately, their house had plenty of room and several empty bedrooms. They had raised a large family. Now their children were all grown and out on their own. Most of their children still lived in the area and had children of their own.

Supper was well attended by numerous family members that had heard Juan was back in town. To start the meal, there had been a spicy corn soup and salad. There were plates of enchiladas, burritos, tacos al pastor and beans. We all talked and ate until we could barely move. It felt like I was back home in Alabama with my own family.

The supper talk was all about the upcoming trip to Chihuahua. It sounded like there would only be a small contingent left in Santa Fe because many of the family members and friends and other residents of the city were intending to go. They made it sound like fun. Juan told me later that many of them would back out before the trip. He said they would get to thinking about their work in town, and the many things they needed to do before winter, then realize they shouldn't go. But they all had fun thinking about what the trip and Chihuahua would be like.

Juan told me the trip would take between twenty to thirty days if there was no trouble, and he certainly didn't expect any. The route to Chihuahua was desolate. There weren't usually any problems in the way of bandits or Indians lying in wait for people to attack. Although that apparently, has happened in the past, so most travelers usually went in groups.

I would leave with Juan from his trading post around December 10th. We would stop by Santa Fe first to gather with the rest of the people who were intending to go. Juan said there might be a couple of different groups. We would plan to get to Chihuahua by early January. After a week or two of trading and eating and singing and dancing, everyone would head back for Santa Fe. Juan says the roughest part of the trip is coming home because it would be well into winter by the time we returned to Santa Fe, and then on to his trading post. However, a great deal of our travels would be in the desert, and not much of anything considered mountains where snow might hamper our travels. All in all, it should be an easy enough journey. I wished there was some way I could talk to Troy about this upcoming trip. He would be as excited as I was.

The talk went late into the evening. Most of it was about Chihuahua, but some of it was about family and friends and the upcoming holiday season. Unfortunately, we would miss that. However, it sounded like there would be some kind of a gift exchange at the house before we left for Chihuahua. There would also be prayers and blessings by the priests at the Cathedral.

"Hey, you ready to have some breakfast?" Juan asked outside the bedroom door trying to get me up.

I could barely roll over. We had stayed up really late. I finally managed to say, "I'm pretty sure I can make it up. Well, then again, maybe I'm not so sure. What's for breakfast? Beans and tortillas?"

"Yes, I'm sure there will be that but there is also likely to be chorizo and tortas left over from last night, and strong coffee."

"Great, I'm getting up," I said. "I just love eating here. Your family makes the best food. I thought I ate pretty good growing up in the hills of Alabama, but nothing like here. Back home we thought chicken and dumplings was pretty near heaven. I would trade a pot of that for anything your mother makes." I threw on my clothes and we headed to the kitchen.

"Bill," Juan's mother started, "What would you like to eat? I have beans, tortillas, eggs, chorizo and tortas?"

I said, "Can I have a little of everything?"

"Certainly, you may," she said excitedly. "Here is some coffee for you to start on and I'll have a plate for you in a few minutes."

Juan and I had breakfast, a pot of coffee and lots of conversation about Chihuahua. We were going to contact some other friends about the trip and then gather some supplies to take back to Juan's place. We planned to be at Juan's trading post for only a few weeks and then head back to Santa Fe.

Our first stop after breakfast was to see Juan's cousin, Manuel. Then our plans were to see Manuel's twin brother, Leon, and his partner Alberto Sanchez. After that we would see the local grocer, Carlos Poso, and then one of the local attorneys, Sid Poso. Sid was a brother to Carlos and a longtime friend of Juan's. It was a cold and beautiful day. You could smell smoke from the chimneys all over Santa Fe. Even with the chill in the air, the scent of pine trees was still strong.

Juan hollered to Manuel as we got to the open door of his blacksmith shop. It was cold outside; but in Manuel's shop it was always warm, because of the fire in the forge. If he wasn't repairing something for a customer, he was busy making knives, belt buckles, bits, and bridles. He also made cast-iron skillets. "Manuel, how are you? Are you planning to go with us to Chihuahua?"

"I'm sure planning too, Juan. A guy can't spend his whole life at a forge. Well, I guess you could. I don't know why you'd want to." Manuel laughed. "Oh, really. I love my work here, especially the forge work; but it would be good to take a break. And I've been spending my spare time making knives that I would like to sell in Chihuahua. And, as usual, I also have some leather goods, bridles and skillets that I would like to take."

"That's great, Manuel. I am really glad you are planning to go. Do you know if Leon is planning to go this year?"

"I don't know, but you can ask him yourself. He is standing behind you," said Manuel.

Leon had walked up behind us without our noticing because of the noise of the forge. Even though Manuel wasn't using it when we came in, it still made considerable noise.

"Leon, you sneaky devil, how are you?" said Juan. They grabbed each other and hugged like two bears wrestling.

When they finally let each other go, Leon said, "I'm doing just about right. How are you?" He also turned to me and shook my hand fiercely. "How are you, Bill? I see you found Juan alright."

"I'm doing great, Leon. It's good to see you. Yes, he wasn't too difficult to find," I said.

"Leon, I assume you are coming with us to Chihuahua and taking some of your new wagons to sell?" Juan asked.

"Yes sir, that is my plan," said Leon. "Hopefully I will have a few wagons that are loaded with items to sell and another wagon with spare parts. Some of the parts are to sell and some in case we need them along the way. And a couple of guys here in town have bought wagons from me to take on the trip. They are carrying goods to sell and hope to fill them back up with things they buy in Chihuahua."

"Good, who else is going with us?" asked Juan.

"Carlos Poso is going," said Leon. "He has several ladies, here in town, that have made shirts and dresses out of all the fabric he bought last year in Chihuahua. He would like to sell those and buy some new clothes and more fabric. He has done well selling his locally made clothes here in Santa Fe but has a lot of leftovers. He would like to take them and see what kind of interest they might attract in Chihuahua."

"Oh, Salman Diaz is also planning to go," Leon remembered. "He has a wagon load of corn meal that he is intending to sell in Chihuahua. He expanded that little mill he used to have and now makes a lot more than he used to. He has a list of things that he wants to buy there and bring back. He is figuring on a full wagon both ways." Leon scratched his head, and then continued, "I talked to Sid Poso the other day and he is planning to go, just for the fun of it." He turned to me and said, "Bill, Sid Poso is a local man that is one of the two attorneys in town. Just like most of the guys going, we grew up with him here in Santa Fe. He is a good man. You'll enjoy getting to know him. He is smart and reads every book he can get his hands on."

I did enjoy getting to know Sid, Carlos and Salman. I told Sid about my ambition to become an attorney someday. He said I would enjoy going to school in Mexico City. I told him I had never been there but hoped to go some day. Juan and I spent the rest of the day talking to them about the trip. We talked about what everyone was taking and when we would leave and when we should expect to get to Chihuahua. Frankly, I was getting more and more excited about the trip. I would like to leave right now, but I knew there was lots of work to do first.

I sure wished that Troy was with me. We had both talked about going to Chihuahua someday. He was aware from his sailing days that lots of merchants shipped goods to Chihuahua and other interior cities in Mexico. They also sent merchandise to coastal cities from Matamoros to as far south as Veracruz. Some of the goods came from a long way away. It made our trip from Santa Fe to Chihuahua sound easy, even though I knew it wouldn't be. Juan had said that it was almost 600 miles and that certainly sounded like a long way to me, especially when we were taking wagons.

We had discussed that it would be closer to ship goods to Santa Fe from U.S. cities once the current war between Spain and Mexico was over. That is one reason I was planning to leave Santa Fe in the spring and go to St. Louis. It would be a long ride and fairly dangerous, but not more dangerous than my trip from New Orleans to Santa Fe. However, I would be the first to admit that I had been extremely lucky to have as little trouble as I did. I was hoping that my luck would last for a lot longer.

Juan and I had supper at Alphonse's hotel with Leon, Manuel, and Sid. We talked all evening about the upcoming trip. Everyone was as excited as I was. Juan was excited about something that I hadn't actually thought about much. He said that everyone going was excellent with weapons. Although no trouble was expected on our trip, Juan said there is always the possibility of bandit or Indian troubles along the way. The thought of being attacked was always present in my mind, but somehow with this big a group I felt more at ease. I guess I shouldn't have.

We finally left the hotel and made it through the cold streets of Santa Fe to Juan's parent's house. The day had been almost warm because the sky had been clear, so there was lots of sunshine. Once the sun went down it turned cold. I kept wondering how cold it might get while we were on our trip to Chihuahua. The fall had been especially warm; but that couldn't hold forever.

The next morning, we ate a quick breakfast of sweet rolls and coffee and were on our way back to Juan's trading post. Before breakfast I had spent some time with Morgan. I had been neglecting him while we were in Santa Fe and tried to make it up to him by giving him a good brushing. Juan had his horse, Red, and the packhorse ready to go by the time I finished brushing Morgan.

As Juan and I rode out of Santa Fe to the north, we both were excited about the trip to Chihuahua. We probably wouldn't have been had we known what the next month would bring.

6 | BACK TO THE TRADING POST

It was a day filled with sunshine and birds singing as we rode through the mountains back to Juan's trading post. Here and there we could smell smoke from the chimneys of Juan's neighbors. He didn't have many neighbors; but there were a few scattered throughout the forest. There was also the occasional campfire belonging to trappers or other people moving through the area. It had been cold lately in the mountains. They were more foothills than mountains, sort of a transition area between where Santa Fe lay and the Sangre de Cristo Mountains to the north and east. About six to eight inches of snow covered the ground. There was absolutely no wind, so it didn't feel as cold as it was. With snow covering not only the ground but all the evergreen trees, it was a sight to remember. I had never seen anything quite like this before. We had the occasional snow in Alabama. They were few and far between though and never lasting long enough to appreciate.

We rode past Carlos' place on our way to Juan's, since it was just off the main path through the area. It looked undisturbed. Juan said he didn't expect any problems, but you never can tell. He said there are far more people traveling through this area than you would think, and not everyone had the best of intentions.

Carlos greeted us as we pulled up our horses in front of the trading post. "Bienvenidos amigos. Estoy muy content de verte."

Juan said, "Carlos, my friend, I am glad to see you also. How have you been? It looks like you have taken good care of my home. Thank you for that."

"I have had a good time," Carlos said. "It has actually been pretty busy. I sold the last two rifles you had in the trading post to a couple of new young trappers along with a couple of blankets and some other odds and ends. I sure hope they will be alright. They had some fairly good equipment; but they didn't seem to know much and were starting too late in the season. I also sold a good bit of food items and a knife, rope, leather straps and another blanket to people passing through. Oh, and I had some Indians come through looking for ponies. I figured they were the ones you had told me about. So, how have you guys been. How was Santa Fe?"

"Santa Fe was like Santa Fe as usual," Juan said with a laugh. "We had a good time visiting with my mother and father and much of the rest of my family. Then we talked to some of the men that will also be going to Chihuahua. My cousin Leon is taking a couple of the wagons he has built and his brother Manuel is taking some of the hand tools and knives he has made. Carlos Poso and his brother Sid are taking a wagon load of the things from his store. Sid is just going to be with Carlos and have a little fun. Salman Diaz is taking a wagon load of the corn meal he has ground in his new mill."

Carlos asked, "Bill, what about you? Did you have a good time?"

I laughed and said, "I certainly did. I think it would be hard to be in Santa Fe without having a good time. It was especially good to meet some of the men going along with us to Chihuahua. Everyone seems excited about the trip. And I'd have to say that I am probably the most excited one. I can't wait to get started."

"I can understand that," Carlos said. "I can still remember the first time I went to Chihuahua. It was to see family. Not for the trade fair. I was a young man and it was really exciting to think about going. After twenty days on the trail some of the excitement had worn off. Oh, but it was still fun. In fact, I loved it. Over the years I went many times; but I don't have any desire to go now. I am too old to take a trip like that. Chihuahua is a young person's trip. I know you will have fun. I will enjoy staying here and watching the trading post while you fellows are gone having a good time. Oh, and speaking of trips, I'd better get on the trail to my place. I'd like to get there before dark. I'll be seeing you soon."

Juan said, "Carlos, you know how much I appreciate your help. I would hate to be gone without you taking care of my home. I look forward to seeing you again soon." They shook hands. And then Carlos and I shook hands and said we would see each other soon. He mounted his horse, Amistoso, and headed down the trail.

Juan and I went to the corral first to check on the horses and mules. We looked them over and they were in good shape. Juan said, "I'm sure glad they are looking healthy. They have no idea what they are going to be in for once we head to Chihuahua. None of these horses or mules have made the trip. Well, my horse, Red, made the trip last year. I've used the pulling horses some in this area and the mules for a couple of longer trips, but none of them on really long trips yet."

I said, "They all look like pretty sturdy animals. If we treat them well, they'll probably be alright. Or at least they should be if we can keep them from breaking a leg or getting hurt in some other way."

Juan said, "You're right there. Injuries for the animals or

any of us can cause a problem. Thankfully the road between Santa Fe and Chihuahua is well worn and shouldn't provide too many problems. Hey, let's go check the house and see about our own food supplies. I'm starting to get hungry."

"That sure sounds good to me," I added.

The house was in good shape as we knew it would be. After a little supper, we worked at resupplying some of the things that Carlos had sold. There were more of at least some of the items in one of the sheds out back. Juan said we would wait until tomorrow to bring up more rifles from the cave under the barn. We had already put away the items we brought on the packhorse from Santa Fe. Then we sat and chatted a while about the trip and went to bed.

After a night's sleep, we both got up feeling better. We were ready to get things done in the next couple of weeks before heading back toward Santa Fe. We would inventory everything that Juan had at the trading post and decide what would stay here and what would go with us to Chihuahua. Juan felt like he always needed to keep certain supplies on hand to satisfy the needs of those travelers, trappers and others that came by the store. Everything else we would load up and take to Chihuahua.

"It's like a juggling act when we go to Chihuahua," Juan said. "I am always both buying and selling. I want to take as many things to sell as possible; but I need to leave enough inventory here to take care of customers. Generally, I take what hasn't been and probably won't be sold, like leftover furs and items I have traded for, but didn't really need. Then in Chihuahua I buy what I think someone in this area might want to buy. This time I am going to take some weapons that I don't particularly like and try to trade them for ones I do like."

Chihuahua, having easier access to the coast and thus merchant ships, had more in the way of manufactured goods and supplies that people would need both on the trail and in town. Of course, Juan's trading post supplied mainly trappers; so guns, knives, traps, clothes, and boots were important. Leather goods, ropes and small hand tools were especially useful on the trail, as were bridles, blankets, and other equipment for horses. This was usually for replacement of items people had broken along the way.

Juan and I spent some time in the barn looking to see how many rifles he still had. We checked to see how much gunpowder and lead there was. We took some of each up to the trading post to replace what had been sold in the last month. Finally, we locked up the rest and made sure to secure the cave, so that nobody would find it. The pile of hay hiding the entrance was getting smaller, but it would be alright, according to Juan. He said, "Even if you took all the hay and swept the floor the entrance was still not easy to see."

I offered, "I bet that's right; because I don't think I could see it and I know that it's there."

"Hey, why don't we go do a little hunting," said Juan. "We should probably see if we can't get a large doe to kill and cure the meat before we take off to Chihuahua. It would keep us from having to hunt along the way."

"Sounds good to me," I said.

With that we were off into the woods. Juan had put a sign on the door to the trading post saying that he would be back by nightfall. There was a place close by the trading post where a small natural pond attracted all kinds of game. It was a refreshing walk up through the woods. There hadn't been any more snow lately and most of the remaining snow had melted. About an hour before sundown, we saw a large doe just before she saw us. Juan finished her with one shot.

We field dressed the doe where she lay and took all the meat back to the trading post. There we cut up the meat into small strips and chunks to cure with a combination of smoke, salt and a few seasonings that Juan liked to use. Juan had created his own smoker that he kept behind the trading post.

Juan got a small fire started in the smoker. We laid the meat on racks to dry. It was salted and put in the smoker. Juan would put more wood in the smoker before we leave in the morning.

The next morning, we ate a quick breakfast and got one of Juan's wagons hitched to his four best mules. He tied his saddle horse, Red, and my horse, Morgan, to the rear of the wagon. We were going to the nearby town for a few additional supplies.

Pojoaque was only a few miles farther to the north from the trading post. It was a small town that had been there for a long time. The town consisted of a store, a blacksmith shop and a church. Juan had a few friends there that he wanted to visit before going on our trip. He said he wanted to "check the weather". That apparently meant he wanted to see how they were and what the "news" of the area was.

We got to Pojoaque before noon. The town didn't have many houses and only a couple of businesses; but it was impressively neat and well cared for. The few families that lived in Pojoaque had been there for years.

We stopped by the church first and talked to Father Marco. He had grown up in Santa Fe and was a long-time friend of Juan and his family.

"Father Marco," Juan called as he saw the priest standing in the doorway of the church. "Oh, it is so good to see you! I was just in Santa Fe recently and everyone told me to tell you they miss you and hope you come that way soon."

The two hugged like they hadn't seen each other in years. Father Marco said, "Juan, I love you and your family. It is so good to see you too. Who is this you have with you, a new convert to the church?"

"No," Juan laughed. "This is Bill Rampy. He's a brother of an old friend of mine. You remember the stories I told you about my sailing days. Well, Bill's brother Troy was one of my fellow sailors. We became best friends and spent many months together exploring the ports along the gulf and the east coast of the United States. Bill came to see me to gain some knowledge about trading in this part of the world. He is staying with me until spring then heading back east. I'll be taking him to Chihuahua soon. That may give him more education than he is looking for."

Father Marco stuck out a big hand and said, "It's a pleasure to meet you, Bill. I certainly hope you enjoy your winter here. It's a beautiful place to live and has a lot of wonderful people, especially Juan's family. They lived just down the road from my family, so I saw them a lot growing up. Oh, and your upcoming trip to Chihuahua, should be quite an education. I hope you enjoy it. What brings you guys to town?"

Father Marco Padilla was about six foot three and weighed probably 250 pounds. He had dark hair and light olive skin. He seemed to be perpetually happy.

Juan answered, "Oh, a couple of things. We are going to stop by the store and get some items to take home with us. But I also wanted to get your opinion on how things are going in the area and whether or not there are any threats to the locals we need to consider or threats on our trip to Chihuahua. Bill and I are going with some of the Santa Fe merchants, so we are certainly not going alone. Carlos is going to be running my place for me while we are gone, so it should be safe. But you never can tell. What have you been hearing?"

Father Marco scratched his head thoughtfully and then said, "I really haven't heard any stories lately that make me worry about our area. Oh, there are always some young bucks from the Apaches that are acting up; but I don't know of any problems near here. On the other hand, what I have heard recently are about things farther south. In fact, you might want to keep an eye open when you head out from Santa Fe toward Chihuahua. I have heard two things. First, there was supposedly a family living south of Santa Fe that recently lost some ponies to a bunch of young Apaches. Nobody was injured, but it did scare them pretty bad. And there have been rumors of some possible bandits down in that same area. It was not clear what they were doing, but they have been seen several times. So far as I know nobody has been attacked. Hey, would you guys like something to drink and to sit a while?"

Juan said, "We would love to. And some of that cake you are famous for wouldn't be bad either if you have some around."

Father Marco said, "You know, I can probably find some of that. Let's go inside and I'll look around."

Father Marco rounded up some fresh coffee and cake, and we went out beside the church to a sunny but protected area. It was surrounded by several pines and a couple of large cottonwoods. Even though it was late fall there were still songbirds singing in the trees. We sat and visited for a good long while. Juan and Father Marco exchanged stories about growing up in Santa Fe. They talked about family and holidays. They also talked about trips down south to see family and about hunting, fishing, and the playing they did as young boys growing up. It reminded me of growing up back in Alabama. My brothers and I would hunt, fish, and play games all day long when we were kids. If we weren't doing any of that, we were target practicing. We actually put so much lead into the hillside behind our targets that our father finally made us dig it all out to reuse.

After a while Juan finally said, "Well, we'd better go see Raoul and then head home. It's always great to see you, Marco. God bless you. We'll see you again after we get back from Chihuahua."

"God bless you, Juan, and you too, Bill," said Father Marco. "I look forward to seeing you again soon."

I said, "I look forward to seeing you too."

And with that Juan and I were off to see Raoul, the local storekeeper. He was another friend of Juan's. But he had not known him nearly as long as he had known Father Marco. Raoul's store provided staple items to locals and others that came through town. He also had some friends that grew beans and sold most of them to Raoul. Juan usually bought large bags of dried beans when he was in town. Raoul had bags of corn meal and bags of salt that Juan bought. Juan also got a selection of other supplies.

We got everything loaded in the wagon and Raoul offered to feed us a quick supper before we went back to the trading post. He said, "Maria has been cooking a large pot of beans all day. You might as well have some. I'll let her know we'll have a few guests for supper and be right back." He headed back into the store and we didn't object.

Raoul came back to the door and waved us both in. He said, "Maria is getting the food on the plates and will holler at us when it's ready. Are you both going to Chihuahua this year?"

Juan said, "Yes, we are. We'll be heading to Santa Fe soon and will meet up with several other people to make the trip. Bill has never been before, so I know he will enjoy it."

"I'm really excited to go," I said. "It sounds like a great adventure. Have you been before?"

"Yes, when I was younger, I went several times," Raoul answered. "You'll want to be extra careful this year from the rumors I have heard. Sounds like several families down that way have had things stolen. Nobody has been injured yet; but you know how that goes. Eventually somebody is likely to get injured or even killed. In the past there have been army patrols down in that area, but not recently. They apparently are too busy fighting down south with those bent on independence. Frankly, I would like to see Mexico be independent; but I hate to see the fight take the soldiers away from the northern areas."

Just then, Maria told us to sit down for supper. We did what she asked. She had fixed a large pot of beans and meat with spices and a few crushed red peppers. She served that along with corn bread and coffee. It was just right for a cool crisp fall day. The coffee was strong and the beans were soft and creamy.

They blended just right with the sweet corn bread.

As we finished supper, Raoul said, "It was good to see you both. We look forward to your return from Chihuahua. Come see us when you get back. We may have a child by the time you get back. I will be taking Maria to Santa Fe soon to spend the rest of the time with her parents. It will be our first. We are both excited."

Juan said, "Congratulations! We will certainly come by here as soon as we get home. May God bless and protect the three of you! See you soon."

They hugged Juan and me tightly. Then we headed back to the trading post. We were barely going to make it there by dark; but it was especially satisfying to have Maria's supper.

All was well at the trading post when we got back. Juan brushed down his horse, Red, and I brushed Morgan. We took care of the mules together. We fed the other animals and made sure they had water. After that we checked the barn and other buildings. Everything was secure. It had been a good day. The weather was still warm and I had a nice time meeting some more of Juan's friends. It wouldn't be long until we were loading up to go meet the others in Santa Fe for our long trip south. It should be a hopefully uneventful trip. However, we did need to warn the others concerning possible danger on the way after what Father Marcos and Raoul had to say.

The next day was a busy one. Several travelers stopped by looking for supplies. We sold some shirts, pants and socks. We also sold one of Juan's remaining coats, two muskets, a rifle, some lead and gunpowder. If trading kept going like this, we might not have much to take to Chihuahua, which would be okay. Juan was more interested in buying stock for his trading post than in selling other items to decrease his inventory.

During the daylight hours, that were certainly getting shorter, Juan and I made sure all the buildings were secure. We were going to be gone for about a month and a half. A lot could happen weather wise in that length of time. It had been a mild fall so far with only a few snows, just enough to keep things looking beautiful in the mountains. There was no telling how long this weather would last.

Juan's hidden cellar in the barn was getting less and less occupied with weapons. Juan had sold most of what he had. Maybe the rumors that Father Marco and Raoul had passed on were getting around and making people decide more weapons might not be a bad idea. We didn't know if the rumors were true; but they appeared to be good for business. However, we intended to be prepared too when heading to Chihuahua.

We started packing the wagons in the barn about a week before our intended departure for Santa Fe. We were going to leave most of the clothes and a few weapons along with some knives, tools and sacks of dried beans and other food. We would take almost everything else with us either for emergencies or to sell once we got to Chihuahua.

Carlos would be coming over in a few days. He would be staying for the duration. He would have his cabin all buttoned up and ready for the winter before he came to the trading post.

7 | BACK TO SANTA FE FOR CARAVAN

By the 5th of December, we were loaded, and Carlos had gotten to the trading post. The wagons had been greased and the horses and mules were in good shape. One of the wagons was about half full of feed and hay for the animals. There were also spare parts for the wagons and harnesses. Juan had traded for several furs over the summer that had been trapped too late to sell in the spring at Taos.

We were also taking some extra weapons, lead and gunpowder. As a hobby, Juan made tools and knives on a small forge he had in a shed attached to the barn. We loaded up many his tools. In addition, we were taking a variety of other things, like ropes, clothes, compasses, and jewelry that Juan thought would sell well in Chihuahua.

The wagons were full, but not too heavy. It shouldn't be enough to require four mules for each wagon; but we thought using four would be a good idea considering how long our trip would be.

The next morning, we had the mules hitched to the wagons and a couple of spare horses tied to the rear along with Morgan and Red. We said goodbye to Carlos and were on our way. Juan drove the lead wagon and I followed with the other wagon.

We took much the same route as I had taken to get here originally. Driving west down through the trees, we came out near the Rio Grande. From there the trail followed the river south. Eventually we met up with the trail that went southeast toward Santa Fe. This was a longer route, and better suited for travel by wagon. It was a long day and we made it to Juan's parents' house in Santa Fe before dark. We had a delicious supper with his parents and then went to bed. We would talk in the morning over a long breakfast; but for now, we both needed some sleep.

I woke up in the morning to the smell of coffee and something wonderful baking in the oven. I got up right away and found that Juan was already in the kitchen talking to his parents. They were telling him the same rumors that we heard from Father Marco and Raoul. They, of course, were concerned and wanted to make sure we were taking the stories seriously. He assured them that we were.

Juan's mother saw me come into the room and said, "Good morning Bill. I hope you had a good night's sleep."

I said, "It was great. I would have stayed in bed longer except for the smell of your coffee and whatever you're baking."

She smiled and handed me a large cup. "Here, I hope you enjoy this as much as the sleep," she said.

I smiled back and said, "I'm sure I will."

Juan said, "Bill, I have been talking to my parents about our trip. They have heard rumors of Indian activity and perhaps bandits also. I assured them that we have some capable people going with us and enough weapons to get due respect for the size of our group. I know for a fact that all of us are good marksmen and good with weapons. I told them that we are not likely to run into any trouble; but if we do, we should be able to handle it. We certainly intend to be cautious."

"I agree, Juan," I said. "We don't anticipate any problems

but certainly expect that we can handle them if they do come." When I said that, I had no idea what was coming my way not that many days in the future.

"Bill, would you like some breakfast?" Juan's mother asked.

"I'd love some," I said.

Juan said, "I'd love some too, Mama."

We would spend the day catching up with the others in our group and seeing if they needed any help getting their wagons and merchandise together. From what we had already heard, everyone was nearly ready to go. One more day should be enough for all of us. Juan and I would help where we could this afternoon and be available in the morning, if needed. Then in the afternoon we would take our caravan of wagons to the Cathedral for a blessing. After the priest's blessing there would be a big supper for everybody going on the trip, and most of their families. The next morning, we would be on our way.

Our first stop after breakfast was to see Juan's cousin Leon. He saw us as we came into his barn where he made his wagons and shouted a greeting. "Buenos Dias, Juan and Bill. Are you guys ready for a little trip?"

"We are," I responded. "But I hear it is more than a "little" trip. How about you? Are you ready?"

Leon laughed and said, "You are right about that. It is more than a little trip. But I'm excited to go. My son, Martin, is staying here to take care of the shop and any repairs that are needed to any customer's wagons. He has been working with me since he was about 12. Now that he is 17, he can pretty much run the place. My friend and partner, Alberto Sanchez, is coming as my co-driver. Alberto and I have known each other our entire lives. It will be great fun to have him with us. We also have four other friends going to drive two more of our wagons. We have them loaded with extra hay and feed for the animals, and a variety of spare parts and equipment. Oh, and we have some spare water barrels, just in case they are needed. Our friends are

Antonio, Jaime, Diego and Jose. We are hoping to sell some of the wagons in Chihuahua."

"Sounds great," I said. "I'm looking forward to meeting them."

Juan and Leon talked a couple of minutes about some family matter. Then Juan and I went to see Leon's twin brother, Manuel, at his blacksmith shop.

"Manuel, how are you?" Juan said as we entered his shop.

"I'm doing fine, Juan," he said. "I'm getting pretty anxious to get on the road for our big adventure."

"Me too," Juan said. "It will be quite a trip. We will make it to Chihuahua and back before you know it. Have you got everything packed and ready to go?"

"I certainly do," Manuel said. "In fact, I had too much ready to go. It made the wagon sit down too low. Leon looked at it and suggested I leave some of my cargo at home. I have taken out a great deal, but it may still not be enough. I'm going to try it the way it is and see if there are any problems."

"Well, if it is still too much we can see if we can put some items in the other wagons," Juan said. "Is everything else going alright?"

"Yes," Manuel said. "Everything is going just right. My son, Benjamin, is staying here to take care of any blacksmithing needs while we are gone. He is just about as good at blacksmithing as I am, so there should be no problems here. My friend, Santiago, is coming along as my co driver."

We told Manuel we would see him later and went over to see Carlos Poso at his store. Carlos was practically running around his store when we got there. Juan said, "Carlos, slow down a minute. What are you doing?"

Carlos went by us without seeing us. Then he heard Juan and stopped. He had an overly excited look on his face at first and then that changed to a smile. He said, "Oh, hi. How are you guys? Sorry, I am distracted this morning, going over what I want to take and what I want to leave in the store. You would think it wouldn't be that hard; but the more I think about it, the more confused I get. I think I'm about done and then something else that either needs to go or stay comes to mind." He laughed and then said, "It really doesn't make that much difference. I'm pretty certain I will sell whatever I take. And then I'll have to decide what to buy and bring back." That gave him another worried look for a minute. He finally relaxed and said, "The wagon is loaded and ready or will be by this afternoon. Hey, Sid is coming as my co-driver. I am excited about that. Even though he and I live in the same town, we don't see each other as much as we should."

Next, we went to see Salman Diaz. It was quiet as we went by his mill, so we looked in the shed behind his house. He looked to be finishing his load and putting a tarp over the wagon. "Buenos Dias, Salman," I said as we came into the barn. "It looks like you are ready to go. Is everything all set?"

"We've got the wagon loaded as heavy as we dare, so I think we're ready," said Salman. "How are you gentlemen?"

"We are ready and it sounds like everybody else is too," I said. "Oh, I'm sure Juan is a little nervous having me as his co-driver." I chuckled. "Is your son, Sebastian, still going as your co-driver?"

"He is," said Salman. "It will be an interesting experience to spend that much time together. I think we will both survive."

"Good," said Juan. "Let me know if you need help with anything and we'll be over. If we don't see you sooner, we will see you tomorrow afternoon at the cathedral."

"See you there," said Salman

Juan and I made a few more stops to see Juan's friends. Then we headed to the hotel for supper with Alphonse and Christine. We had a wonderful visit and then went to Juan's parents' house for the night. It would be a busy day tomorrow.

Juan and I got up about the same time. We could smell his

mother's cooking and coffee. The aroma had filled the house and was irresistible, so it didn't take us long to get to the kitchen. Juan's mother and father were both there helping each other. His mother was frying fresh tortillas and his father was stirring a large pan of refried beans.

Juan patted his father on the back and hugged his mother. He said, "How are you two today? It looks like you are going to feed us well, as usual."

Juan's father said, "Yes, we thought we had better feed you well this morning because it will be a while before we get to do it again."

There seemed to be a little nervousness in his voice, so I suspected they were also thinking about how dangerous this trip might be. Juan and I had talked about this some. We felt like we would be fairly safe. We had seven wagons pulled by mules and extra horses going on the trip, plus fourteen men. Our group would look impressive enough that we should be left alone by anybody or any group that wanted to do us harm. If we were attacked by a group of Indians or bandits, we had considerable fire power. Each man would have a pistol plus two rifles. In addition to that. we had lots of extra lead balls, flint, and gunpowder. We all knew that nothing would keep us completely protected from harm, but we were trying to do our part to keep the odds in our favor.

Juan and I chatted with his parents as we enjoyed their warm and invigorating breakfast. Then we headed out to see everybody one more time in case anybody needed extra help.

It was a chilly morning. The sun seemed promising for warming things up well by afternoon. We enjoyed riding around Santa Fe to see everyone. As usual, the air was full of the smell of pines and chimney smoke. A light coating of snow that had fallen overnight blanketed the ground; but it should be gone soon.

At about mid-afternoon our entire group, along with their

wagons, mules, extra horses and gear assembled at the Cathedral for a blessing from the priest for safety and success in our journey. Everyone in our group regularly attended the Cathedral except for me. They were all familiar with this kind of church function. It would be a first for me.

Juan told me there would be a ceremony and prayers performed by the priest in the name and with the authority of the Church. He said the purpose was for all the persons and things to be sanctified as dedicated to Divine service and perhaps marked with some Divine favor.

The anticipation of leaving was getting everyone excited, especially me. I'm not sure why, but I just had the feeling that something special was going to happen on this trip. Not necessarily to me, but to some of us or at least one of us. Unfortunately, I also had a slight feeling of dread, like something bad might happen. Time would tell, I assumed.

Our group was impressive once we all came together. With the extra horses tied on the back of each wagon, plus the mules in front pulling the wagons, our group stretched down one entire side of the square as we moved toward the Cathedral.

At the Cathedral, the priest was waiting for us along with an assistant and two nuns. Father Estrada had been in Santa Fe for many years and was well known and loved by everyone in town. He was a distinguished looking man with silver hair. His vestment was black with several pieces and some slight ornamentation. His assistant was a younger priest. He wore vestments that looked less formal. The two nuns wore black habits with black and white coifs on their heads.

Juan introduced me to almost everyone there, even though it was a large group of people. There were a few minutes of talk and smiles and then the ceremony began. Our group lined up together in one line in front of the wagons. Father Estrada walked first along our wagons, mules, and horses as he prayed. Then he walked in front of our group and prayed for each of us individually. After that he centered himself in front of the group and talked to us in a friendly, but serious way. He said, "Friends, I have known most of you since you were children. You know that I love you all and your wonderful families. It is my great blessing to have served here in Santa Fe with you for these many years. I asked our Father in Heaven to protect you all on your trip and make your trip successful. I prayed for safety on the trip for you and your families while you are gone. It is my pleasure to know you all and I await your safe return from Chihuahua. I wish I could go with you, so that I could worship in their beautiful Cathedral. It has been many years since I was there last. May God bless and keep you all."

Father Estrada shook hands with each of us and said he would see us at supper. I was moved almost to tears by the ceremony and prayers. It was not like anything I had ever been involved in before. I thought if anything could protect us along our trip, his prayers and the prayers of these good people were probably it.

Three men that I had not met came over to speak to Juan, Leon, and Manuel as soon as the ceremony was over. They greeted each other warmly and chatted for several minutes. There smiles on each face at the end of the conversation. They shook hands and the men left. I had no idea what they had talked about; but it turns out that it was probably an answer to one of Father Estrada's prayers.

After the visiting was over, all the wagons were taken to Manuel's shop. We unhooked the mules and horses and let them loose in his corral. A few of the wagons went into the barn and the rest had been put by the corral. We would take turns watching the wagons during the evening since they were all loaded with goods of considerable value.

Before we left the corral, Juan called us all together and told us that he had been approached by the leaders of another group that was about to head to Chihuahua. They suggested we all go together so that we would have a larger group and more guns in case anything happened along the trail. Everyone was in favor of teaming up with the other group. Most of the men in the other group were well known to our group. Considering the rumors and common concerns about danger on the trail, everybody was excited and knew that their families would be also.

In the evening, the friends and family of everyone going on the trip hosted a fiesta style meal just outside the Cathedral. It was quite a party. Back home in Alabama, we occasionally had a big party to celebrate a wedding or birth; but they were nothing like this. There was food and food and more food. And after the food was gone and the dishes cleaned up, there was music and dancing. It was a great deal of fun. I loved the excitement of the music. There were four guitar players playing all together. I had never seen dancing like this before, so eventually a couple of young ladies came over to get me to dance. I tried it and had a good time, but I certainly didn't do it well.

Juan caught me at a break and said, "Bill, you seem to be having a good time. I thought you told me you couldn't dance."

I replied, "Do you think I was really dancing? I thought I was just holding on for dear life. I was trying not to fall down or make somebody else fall down. But it was fun anyway. Hey, it looked like you were having a good time too."

"Yes," Juan said. "I have been having a nice time. You know how important my family is to me. I can't think of anything I enjoy more than a fiesta with my family. And this one is especially enjoyable because almost everyone is here."

As the fiesta started to wind down, all of us that would be in tomorrow's caravan had a short meeting about watching the wagons and when we would gather to leave in the morning. Then we left to get some sleep. I had the first shift watching the wagons. Juan relieved me after an hour or so. I had my bedroll in the wagon, so I went to the corral and bedded down by Morgan. I really had been ignoring him lately, so would get up early in the morning to feed and brush him well.

Everyone began to assemble just before the sun came up. All the horses and mules were fed and made ready for the day. The mules were hooked up to the wagons. The horses were tied up to the back of the wagons. Juan's mother had brought a large pot of refried beans and fresh tortillas for everyone to snack on while they were getting ready to go.

The other group of men got to the cathedral about the same time as our group. They had more men and animals than we did. There were eight wagons pulled by mules. Each wagon had two drivers with a horse or two tied to the back. In addition, there were several horses and riders who were leading a packhorse or two loaded with cargo. This group had not intended to depart for another couple of days. When they heard we were leaving, their leaders decided it would be much safer to go with us. It appeared that we would all remain as two separate organizations, but just travel together. That did sound like an answer to prayer to me. Even I had started to get a little nervous about the size of our group once everyone else did. Our new bigger group of men would certainly be safer. It would take a large band of Indians or bandits to want to attack us.

8 | BOUND FOR CHIHUAHUA

You could feel the excitement. Everyone was ready to take off for Chihuahua. The air was cool and fresh. Frost was over all the trees and shrubs. There were piles of snow here and there where it had drifted up during the last snow. Other than that, the ground was clear. It was going to be a beautiful day to start a long trip. Even the birds were singing, although, I doubted that was because of our impending departure.

Since we were still near the Cathedral, Father Estrada came out and wished us all well. He greeted the new additions to our group and said prayers over them individually. He knew all of them well. He said one last prayer over the entire group for our trip. Then our caravan was off on the road to Chihuahua.

Juan's group was leading the way on the first day. Juan drove the first wagon and I followed him in the second wagon. Red was tied to the back of Juan's wagon, along with a spare horse. Likewise, my horse Morgan was tied to the back of my wagon along with a spare horse.

Juan had arranged for two of his nephews to be our co-drivers. Lorenzo was riding with me and Luis was riding with

Juan. They were sons of Juan's oldest sister, Isabella. They were twins, about twenty years old, and looked so much alike, that I couldn't tell them apart. Both young men were trim and almost six feet tall.

Lorenzo and Luis had never been to Chihuahua before. Juan had been telling them since they were kids that he would take them some day. Their day had finally come and they were excited. Juan said he was proud to be their uncle because they are fine young men. I could tell already that they were going to be an asset to our caravan.

We were heading south through Santa Fe but would eventually turn southwest toward La Cienega. There was a small pueblo there that we wouldn't be visiting. The area had several springs where we could stop for the night and refill our water barrels. That would be our first stop. It was about a twenty-mile ride. We were hoping to average more than twenty miles per day, so this day would be both a test and a time to check all the wagons. One good day on the trail would give us an opportunity to see if there were going to be any problems. Almost everyone had a wagon built by Leon. They were sturdy and should do well.

It was a beautiful day. The sky was clear and the air crisp. You could see and smell smoke coming out of all the chimneys along the trail as we left Santa Fe. There were quite a few people out moving around. I suppose many of them were just looking at our caravan. Our group being as large as it was must have drawn a lot of interest. As the road began to turn southwest on the edge of town, I looked back and got a good look at our caravan. It was an impressive group of wagons, people, and animals.

As we got out of town Juan picked up speed a little with his wagon. The route had been traveled many times and was especially smooth at this point. We were traveling southwest and slightly downhill. The road was still in a wooded area. Most of the trees were green because they were pines, cedars and a few other varieties of evergreens. There were other trees that had already dropped their leaves. Most of them were aspens. They had been especially beautiful until all the leaves were gone. Their leaves had been an unusually bright yellow. I had never seen an aspen until I came to Santa Fe. My home state of Alabama had plenty of trees, but no aspens as far as I knew.

I asked Lorenzo, "What do you and your brother do, Lorenzo? Have you been working for your father or are you going to school?"

"We have been working on our family's ranch with our father." He smiled and said, "Our whole lives have been spent in Santa Fe and on the ranch. We have been thinking though about starting school soon. The ranch is a good way of life, and we enjoy it; but we want to look at other possibilities."

I said, "I completely understood. Life is a journey for many of us. We want to look at other things to do or places to go. Your Uncle Juan had his journeys earlier in his life, and of course, I am actually on a journey now. So, I wish you both well in whatever paths you take."

"Thank you," he said. He had a big smile on his face. I'm sure it wasn't from what I had said, probably more from thinking about whatever step they were about to take.

After being on the road for about two hours, we stopped to give everybody a short break. Then we continued on. Everyone seemed to be in good spirits. There was even someone singing from time to time. Most of the singing was corridos, which told of historical events. A few favorite corridos talked of the Mexican War for Independence that was currently underway. Other corridos were love songs about wives and families.

The singing made me think of Troy and our days back home in eastern Alabama. There had been lots of singing while we were growing up. We sang at home and would also sing when we got together with other neighbors for worship services. Troy and I were both tenors. Our dad was the family bass. We sang hymns from an old church hymnal we had at home. A small independent Christian church was near our home and we almost grew up there because of the music. Our family would have loved the corridos.

We stopped for a quick lunch a couple of hours after the first stop. Juan and I made it back along the line of wagons to check on how everything was going so far. The general feeling was that things were going smoothly. There were no mechanical problems and everyone was feeling good.

Since everyone had heard rumors about possible Indian and or bandit attacks, every driver was looking for signs of trouble. Nobody had seen anything yet. We really were hoping the size of our group would keep attackers away from us. Every driver had at least two guns close at hand and knew how to use them.

After another break in mid-afternoon, we got into the area of La Cienega. There were several springs nearby. Juan, and a couple of the other guys who were experienced on the trail, picked where they wanted to stay for the night. We stopped at an area that was well out in the open. It was where nobody would be able to sneak up to our camp unless they came on foot, and that was not likely. We pulled the wagons into an oval shape and got the wagons close enough to make sort of an animal pen. All the animals were fed and watered and put into our makeshift corral. Some of the riding horses were tied in strategic areas around the pen; because there may be a need to get saddled and ride out in case of attack.

A couple of campfires were built in the middle on the circle. All of the men knew each other, so they mixed well on this first night. I was glad to see that. It looked like it would be a friendly bunch.

Juan came over to where I had squatted down by one of the fires and said, "Bill, how did your first day on the Chihuahua trail go?"

I laughed and responded, "I thought it was great fun. I had

a nice time visiting with your nephew Lorenzo. He is an intelligent young man. How did you like the way things went?"

Juan said, "I was pleased that we made such good time. It would be nice if we could do this all the way to Chihuahua. And, although that may be a bit much to ask for, I am hoping for it all the same. I was glad that we didn't see any sign along the way of the movement of anything other than individuals or small groups. I really thought we might see more."

After a while everyone started settling down for the night. Some were getting in between the two campfires. The fires had been fed a little more wood to keep the fire going longer.

Juan, and the leader of the other group, Pablo, got together and set up a watch rotation. I was going to take the first watch from our group. Manuel would take watch after me, and Leon after him. It promised to be a good night. It was crisp, but not too cold. There was little breeze most of the time.

Just as things were starting to settle down, and before anyone had gone to sleep, there was a bright light in the western sky. It was like nothing I had ever seen before. We could see that it was moving from north to south. It was dropping in the sky. As it got closer to earth it seemed to be on fire. Then some of it broke up into many little burning balls.

All of us were watching it. As it got closer to the ground, it wasn't far from our camp. When it did finally hit, we could feel the ground shake. We could see no more flame after it hit. I thought surely it would catch some of the brush on fire, but it didn't.

I could hear some of the men talking about what it was. Some of them were afraid it was a ghost. Others thought it might be somebody or something from the sky that had come to attack us. Whatever it was, nobody slept well that first night. It certainly gave all of us something to talk about for the rest of the way to Chihuahua.

I tried to get to sleep after my turn on guard, but I couldn't.

Every time I would start to relax, I would hear a noise of some kind out in the brush and I would lay there expecting something to happen. Nothing ever happened and I never got to sleep.

The next morning it was pretty clear from the conversation around the fires that everyone had the same amount of sleep that I did. I was thinking that everyone would be taking a siesta during the lunch break.

After the fires were put out and the animals fed and watered, we were ready to go. The other group's leader, Pablo, was going to take the lead today. His group would follow him and we would follow them. We were intending to keep this rotation up all the way to Chihuahua.

Pablo was about six feet tall. He was stocky and had a big booming voice that made him sound like a natural born leader. His people all seemed to have a great deal of respect for him, so I think he was the natural leader that his voice seemed to indicate.

Juan didn't have the booming voice that Pablo did; but our group and the other group all had a lot of respect for him. Both men had some of the same natural leadership characteristics which would obviously be helpful over the next month and a half.

Juan and I decided to ride together this day. That would let Luis and Lorenzo ride together. Our next stop should be about halfway between La Cienega and the village of Albuquerque. There would supposedly be a few rough, rocky patches on the trail today. However, most of the road would be well worn and relatively easy. Our route today was along the Santa Fe River. It would eventually flow into the Rio del Norte River. We would follow that river for most of the way to Chihuahua.

"Juan, tell me about when you and my brother Troy met," I asked after we got moving down the trail. "I can't believe you and I have known each other this long and I have never asked you about that."

Juan smiled and started, "As I recall we met in Yorktown, Virginia at a boarding house run by a lady named Margaret Phillips. She was a wonderful cook and an outgoing person. I had been there a couple of days and Troy had just gotten there.

"We had both heard that we might be able to get a job sailing with a merchant ship named the 'Willa Mae'. The 'Willa Mae' regularly sailed up and down the coast carrying all kinds of goods from port to port. The captain apparently lived at Yorktown, so he would stop there on a regular basis. He would spend a few days with his wife, replenish his crew and sail on down the coast. Troy and I had both heard that we might be able to get a job with him the next time he was in port.

"Troy had been there before and had already heard the story about the 'Willa Mae'. He had ridden from Alabama through Georgia and the Carolinas to Virginia. I think he was intending to go farther north until he decided it would be interesting to sail up or down the coast on a merchant ship. He had been to Yorktown before because it was one of the places he wanted to see. He had heard that during the Revolutionary War, a unit from his grandfather's hometown, Zweibrucken, Germany, had fought with the United States in that area. Zweibrucken was right on the border between France and Germany. It supposedly had been a part of each country at different times."

With a surprised look on my face, I said, "Wow Juan, I had never heard that before. I did know that our grandfather had come from Germany, or maybe it was France. I wasn't sure about the name of the town. And I had certainly never heard about their soldiers helping our soldiers. That is interesting. I did know that our grandfather apparently changed his name when he came to this country. His name was originally Rempe, but he changed it to Rampy. I've never known why."

"I think Troy told me that story too," said Juan. "I don't think he knew why the name was changed either; but I understand it was pretty common to change one's name when moving to a different country. So far as I know my family didn't change their name when they moved from Spain; but I don't know for sure. I've never heard it spoken about."

"Did you and Troy get on a ship pretty soon in Yorktown?" I asked.

"We were in Yorktown about a week before the "Willa Mae" got back to port. Then it had a layover for another week. So, Troy and I had about two weeks to get to know each other. We had a good time telling each other about our lives and family. He invited me to northeastern Alabama and I invited him to Santa Fe. Some of our life stories were so similar that it really drew us together. We spent time in the local area, just riding around, seeing the countryside and visiting all the small towns. We had in mind going further up the coast but decided we didn't have enough time.

When they started filling the crew for the "Willa Mae" we were both hired right away, even though neither of us knew much about sailing. It was not that difficult after all, so we found our jobs interesting and exciting. The first thing we learned was how to load the ship. Even though the "Willa Mae" was not considered a large ship it certainly seemed to hold a lot of merchandise. In an enclosed area on the upper deck, we loaded cattle and horse feed, furniture, boots, dishes, clothes and all kinds of odds and ends for storekeepers along the way. "

"Did you sail south down the coast at that time?" I asked.

"No, we actually headed north toward New York City at first," said Juan. "The ship's captain had received a load at Yorktown that was livestock and the owners wanted them shipped to New York City. They had heard that the demand for meat was growing rapidly. And, of course, the price people were willing to pay was also increasing. We were taking almost an entire ship loaded with sheep, in the lower hold. That was about the time the captain decided he needed Troy and I because we both knew something about livestock. The rest of the crew knew sailing, but not animals. Troy and I spent some time learning to sail, but mostly we took care of the sheep. It was our job to make sure they arrived in New York in good health. We must have done a good job; because when we got to New York City all the animals were still alive and in decent shape."

"How long did you stay in New York City? Did you get to see anything more than the port?"

"We did get to see a little, mainly the area around the port," Juan said. "The captain thought it would take three or four days to arrange a new load, so he was willing to give everybody leave once we got the cargo hold cleaned up. The sheep really didn't make much of a mess. It had been smooth sailing most of the way, so they didn't get seasick. Troy and I did; but that's a different story. I think the rest of the crew spent their time on the dock where there were places to eat and drink. Troy and I spent most of our time walking around the business area near the dock. The shops were interesting. Some sold a variety of clothes while others sold household goods and hardware items. That's probably what started Troy thinking about having his own store."

"I'll have to ask him about that someday," I said.

Our caravan stopped about mid-day for a rest break. All the animals were watered and fed. Some of us took a quick siesta. Pablo had picked a place to stop near some large cottonwood trees for shade. We were still by the Santa Fe River, so water was plentiful. There were pines and aspens also in front of us; but it was fairly open to the east.

We had been keeping our eyes open to see if there were signs of groups in the area, such as clouds of dust, that might signal the possible presence of either Indians or bandits. Nothing had been seen so far. Soon we were back on the trail.

After our break, I wanted to continue Juan's stories about sailing so I asked him where they went after they left New York City.

He said, "After about four days the captain let us know that a new load was coming and we should return to the ship. The load was a variety of things a large merchant wanted taken to Boston. It took the crew about a day and a half to load the cargo. We set sail the next day.

"It was a beautiful sail to Boston. The wind was strong enough to carry us along at a good pace and it was from the right direction. I think it took about three days to get there and unload. It took a few days for the captain to get a new load. The load was shoes and boots, as I recall. Oh, there was some printing equipment too and some lumber. It was only a partial load; but the captain thought we should sail. The weather had changed and was looking like it might get rough. We were sailing back to New York and the captain wanted to get ahead of the weather. He sure knew what he was talking about because it did get rough. Neither Troy nor I had ever seen weather like that and especially not on a ship. It was making both of us think that our sailing careers might be short lived. At that point, Troy and I just wanted to get back to dry land. Thankfully, the captain and several of the crew were experienced and they got us back to New York without any major problems."

"I can't imagine what sailing would be like on a good day much less on a bad day," I said. "I really think that might have scared me bad enough that I wouldn't ever want to sail again."

"Oh, it was pretty bad," Juan said. "But after we got to New York and unloaded the cargo, the captain gave us all several days off. After that, we were off several more days getting a load. By the time we got a new load and got it stowed aboard the ship, Troy and I must have been ready to go again. It didn't hurt that the weather had gotten back to normal and was really beautiful again. We sailed down the coast dropping off cargo and picking up cargo for some time. We stopped at six or eight little ports. Some of the bigger ones we stopped at were Norfolk, Wilmington, Charleston and then Savannah."

"Sounds like you guys must have had an interesting time,"

I said. "Well, with the exception of the stormy weather. I'm not sure I would care for that. Travelling on solid ground is more to my liking, I think. It seems to be quite a bit safer. Well, except for the occasional Indian or bandit attack. And so far, I have been pretty lucky in that regard."

We stopped for the night on a flat area near the river. The caravan continued to form an oval shaped corral at night for protection and to keep the animals corralled. Our corral was bigger than one would think, because not only were the wagons long at fifteen feet, but they also had long tongues that gave the rigs another ten feet. The mules and horses were tied to the inside of their individual wagons. That left the center of the corral open for campfires and an area for bedrolls.

We usually had two campfires a little way apart. The two groups were mixing fairly well since most of the men knew each other. It was another beautiful night. You could see stars in every direction in the sky. There were no clouds and only a sliver of moon. With most men sitting near the fires as they ate supper, there was even some singing. Someone had brought a guitar and was quite talented. It had been an especially good day.

I stood watch that night about three in the morning till four. It was quiet and the sky was still filled with stars. I couldn't help wondering just how many there were. I was pretty sure I couldn't count that high. I saw many constellations I had learned from my father when I was young. I could see Orion, Gemini, Canis Minor and Canis Major in the southwest. There was Sextans, Hydra, Antlia, and Leo Minor in the south. And then there was Corvus and Virgo in the southeast. Of course, the moon was also in the southern part of the sky. It was cold, but not uncomfortable sitting by one of the fires with my clothes on and my blanket wrapped around me. It was a spectacular night.

While we were on watch at night, and riding in our wagons during the day, everyone kept looking for any sign of other riders in the area. Any travelers going our direction would be traveling the same path as we were. Anybody else traveling the same direction, but not on the established path, might be trying to follow us and perhaps attack us at some inconvenient spot. So far nothing threatening had been seen.

When my relief took over at 4:00 am, I just stayed up and went to check on Morgan. He was doing well, although I'm sure he would rather me ride him than be tied to the back of the wagon. I talked to him quietly and rubbed him down good with a rough piece of burlap.

I made myself a cup of coffee over the hot coals left from one of the fires. The fire had been fed some wood throughout the night in order to keep warmth going.

Both groups were up quickly and got their gear, mules, and horses ready to go. It should be a short day. Tonight's stop would be Albuquerque and it probably wasn't a full day's ride. Some of the men in both groups had family in Albuquerque that they might want to see. We probably wouldn't actually go through town and would spend the night on the outskirts. Those of us who didn't have relatives there would stay with the wagons and animals. We would be close enough to town that everything should be safe, even without guards. However, we didn't intend to take any chances.

Juan was the leader of both groups today. He and I rode again in his wagon. Pablo and his group brought up the rear of the caravan. They would keep a lookout for any signs of other riders following us or riding off to the right or left. The river was to our right, so any attack today would have to come from our left. However, we were still thinking that the size of our group would prevent anyone from attacking the group as long as it was together. We should have thought that through better.

The land we rode over was smooth on our side of the river. The other side was considerably rougher, so it was good that we were on this side. The wind came up more in the late morning, then calmed down by the afternoon. We didn't take a mid-day break because everyone was anxious to get to Albuquerque.

By early afternoon we were there. Juan and Pablo had talked about where they wanted to camp for the night. The spot was right on the edge of the village, so it would be convenient for those wanting to go see their relatives or friends.

We had learned from our first two nights on the road to drive into our camping position first and then water the mules and horses later. That got done quickly this evening. Then anyone wanting to go into town let it be known to Juan or Pablo, so they could set up a watch list. Everyone was supposed to be back to camp by at least two hours after dark.

About half of the men were going to stay in camp instead of going to see friends or relatives. Juan and I rode into the village just so I could see what it was like. Juan had been here many times and he thought I would like to see it.

Our camp was adjacent to what appeared to be the main street in Albuquerque. Juan said we should ride through the village a few miles and then come back. It felt good to have Morgan and Red saddled up again. I think they enjoyed our ride as much as we did. We discussed that we probably should take turns riding along with the caravan as sort of a scout to investigate anything that looked suspicious. I would take the first turn in the morning.

The village of Albuquerque appeared to be much larger than Santa Fe. It was attractive, with many adobe homes and buildings. Most of them were a natural earth color. Some had painted trim around the windows and under the roof lines. All the roofs were flat.

The village was named after Francisco Fernandez de la Cueva, Duke of Albuquerque. The title was a hereditary title in the Peerage of Spain.

The elevation wasn't high in the foothills like Santa Fe. Even though it was close to a forested area, where it lay was more of a high desert.

We saw several cafes, several clothing stores, and three or four general merchandise shops. From what I knew of Albuquerque's location, it must be a crossroads of sorts. I imagined it would be a good place for business. All the businesses we had seen were proof of that. This looked like a prosperous place to set up a shop, like Troy had done in New Orleans. Not that Troy was looking for another location; but who knows what could happen in the future?

"This looks like a busy town, Juan. Maybe Troy should expand his empire here someday," I said with a little chuckle.

"It is a busy town and an especially good location," Juan responded. "It will probably be a large city in the future. I definitely think Troy should expand his business empire here."

"Have you spent much time in Albuquerque," I asked?

"I have more family that live in town," he said. "So, we do get down here occasionally for holidays. I have always enjoyed it. We get to Albuquerque far more often than Chihuahua since it is so much closer to Santa Fe. Hey, maybe we'd better get back to camp and get a good night's sleep. I think tomorrow will be a rougher ride with the wagons."

I laughed and said, "I'm glad I will be playing scout tomorrow. Riding Morgan will be easier than that wagon seat."

Off in the distance we heard a high lonely howl that I couldn't identify. I asked, "What is that?"

Juan said, "Oh, that's probably a lobo or gray wolf. It's probably the meanest non-human thing around here. But it shouldn't come anywhere near our camp."

We returned to camp, unsaddled the horses and brushed them down. Then we went to bed anticipating a tough day on the road tomorrow.

I got up easily in the morning. Even though we had not gotten to bed early last night, I was still refreshed and ready to get on the road. Everyone checked and rechecked their equipment and refilled their water barrels. From here onwards, the road to

Chihuahua would get rougher and more desolate. There were some small villages along the way; but they couldn't provide anything in the way of supplies. However, our supplies and water were in good shape. The caravan would probably camp near Los Lunas tonight. There should be a well there. Every time we got a chance, we would refill our barrels. There could be days ahead when we wouldn't be able to find water on the trail, so we needed to be ready.

Morgan and I had a good visit about the day ahead as I rubbed him down and got him saddled. I think he was ready for a good ride with just the two of us. I ate a little breakfast, talked to Juan about the day, and then rode out ahead of the caravan. Juan was going to drive the wagon by himself. Louis and Lorenzo would be together.

Morgan and I eased out of camp just as the caravan began to move. I would go east away from the river to find high ground as a lookout. After I watched from that location for a while, I would move parallel to the caravan. I would watch from there for about an hour. Then I would find another area of high ground to sit and watch. If I could see a likely spot to cross the river, I would cross and do the same thing on the other side.

After I had paralleled the caravan for a while, I did see a likely location for crossing the river. I moved out to that area and was able to get across the river. I eased up into the hills to see what I could. Frankly, I didn't see anything. I didn't want to get overconfident. I continued in this pattern for the rest of the day until we stopped for the night near Los Lunas.

Los Lunas was a small town that had apparently been part of a land grant over 100 years earlier to the Luna family.

We stayed on the outskirts of town. Nobody went into town that night. Juan, Luis, Lorenzo, and I just sat and talked about the day and what tomorrow should bring. There had been no problems and we continued to see no evidence of anyone paralleling or following us. I certainly hoped it stayed that way.

Tomorrow night we would camp near either La Joya or possibly Socorro if the traveling was easy. Juan on Red would do the scouting in the morning. We went to bed early thinking that it could be a long day.

9 | TROUBLE ALONG THE WAY

The next morning everyone was ready to go early. Luis, Lorenzo, and I got our two wagons ready to go while Juan saddled Red. As the group started to move out, we fell in line behind them. I was driving one wagon and Luis and Lorenzo were continuing to drive the other one together. They were doing a good job and seemed to be enjoying the trip, so far.

Pablo was leading again. He recalled that this next stretch of trail was fairly rough from rocky ground, so he didn't intend to go any faster than a walk. But he would move out when he could; because he still wanted to move as fast as we reasonably could.

Many things could make a trail rough. Of course, if the trail crossed rocky ground, there was nothing that could be done to make it smooth. Sandy soil made the best trails most of the time. If they were wet, they wouldn't get sticky and muddy and if they were dry, they were smooth. The only problem with sand was if the loose sand was too deep it could bog down the wagons. Clay soils were bad when wet because they made mud that could be a serious problem. When dry, clay soils were usually alright.

However, if they got too dry, they would get rough from clods of dirt getting thrown up and making holes in the trail.

The trail this day certainly was rougher than normal. By the time we stopped for a break around noon, one of the wagons in Pablo's group was having some trouble. The driver of that wagon, Jose, and his co-driver, Alejandro, would stay behind with Leon and Alberto to let them work on the wagon. They would hope to catch up with the caravan soon. I stayed with the four of them to keep watch while they worked. We hadn't seen Juan during the break; but assumed he wasn't too far away.

Leon and Alberto worked about a half hour to get the wagon repaired. It had been a minor problem with the suspension under the front of the wagon. Just as Jose and Alejandro were about to pull out to get back on the trail, we all heard loud shouts from the trees to our east. Suddenly, about ten ponies and Indian braves rushed out of the trees, no more than 100 feet away.

Even though we were always aware that something like this could happen, when it did it was startling. All ten riders released arrows as they rode toward us. Their attack was sudden and deadly.

The first hail of arrows did not seem particularly accurate; but it was shocking anyway. We were not able to get to our weapons until they already had their second arrows on the way.

Unfortunately, the first arrows were more accurate than we had thought. Jose and Alejandro were sitting on the wagon ready to pull away when the attack started. They were each hit by some of the first arrows and both fell over into the wagons. It was not possible to determine how badly they had been wounded, but it looked as if they could be seriously injured.

Leon, Alberto, and I were able to find protected spots and fire back at the riders. Jose and Alejandro were unable to fire back at the braves.

As the Indians charged toward us, they were all able to lose two arrows each by the time they got to us. It was apparent to them that we were starting to fire. Their ponies seemed to pick up speed and ran past us. We fired after them and only injured one brave. They turned, thinking they were out of range, and started back toward us to attack again.

The braves were Apaches according to Leon and Alberto. It wasn't clear how they had been able to sneak up on us. Our guess was that they came up a narrow valley to the east and behind us about a half mile. They probably saw some of our dust and came up to see how big of a group we had. When they saw only three wagons, we probably seemed easy to attack. I assume they wanted to finish us all and take the wagons and gear or maybe just the gear.

Unfortunately for the braves, they were not completely out of range when they turned around. We got in some good shots at that point. Two of them fell from our first series of shots and two more fell as they charged toward us. Added to the first one that fell earlier, we had disabled half of their war party before they got back to us the second time. But they were still pressing their attack. The three of us had another weapon apiece ready by the time they were close to us.

I had my Henry 1813 flintlock pistol loaded and ready. It apparently had been made for the U.S. Navy by Joseph Henry in Philadelphia. Troy gave it to me when I was heading toward Santa Fe. I'm not sure where he got it, but I assume he traded something for it.

I liked the pistol a great deal. It felt good in my hand, shot straight, and was easy to load. I always kept the charge and ball ammunition and a ramrod within quick reach. That certainly came in handy today.

Leon and Alberto both got off shots with their rifles and it appeared they both wounded braves. I waited until a brave was practically on top of me and fired. He must have fired at the same time. I could feel the impact of his arrow in my chest. The shock of it must have knocked me out because I don't remember any more of the fight.

When I awoke, it was dark, and I was laying on my bedroll near one of the campfires. Juan was sitting close to me talking to Leon and Alberto. They heard me stirring and all came over to talk to me.

Juan said, "Bill, how do you feel? I'm glad to see you awake. That was quite a fight you had."

I said, "To be right honest with you, I feel fortunate to be alive. How's everybody else? How are Jose and Alejandro?"

Juan looked stricken when I asked that. Then he said, "Neither one of them made it." He choked up for a minute and then continued. "Jose was hit with an arrow in the center of the chest and must have died almost instantly. Alejandro was hit in the stomach and bled to death, before any of us could get to him and try to stop the bleeding. Leon said they were sitting on the wagon ready to pull out when the attack started. I guess they provided too good of a target for the braves. Most of the first arrows must have gone toward them. It's a wonder they weren't hit more than once apiece. But I guess once was enough anyway. I feel terrible about losing them."

I asked, "What did they do with their bodies? Were they buried here?"

Alberto said, "They were both from Albuquerque, so Pablo sent five of his men to take their bodies back there. He thought the family would like to be able to bury them there."

Juan said, "The trip there and back should go quickly, so I told Pablo we would wait here until they get back."

I looked at Leon and said, "Tell me about the rest of the fight after I got hit."

Leon started to talk and then choked up. Then he continued, "After you shot the brave that hit you, things were pretty much over. The brave you hit was dead, as were at least three more. Most of the rest of them were wounded. About that time, Juan came riding in along with about five more of our men. I think the braves had given up by that time; but when they saw the others coming up the road, they really took off. They gathered the wounded and headed east as fast as they could go."

"Who doctored me?" I asked. "And how bad was the wound?"

"Carlos doctored you," Leon said. "He said you should be alright, if he got your wound clean enough. There is a special liquid he used for cleaning the wound. He had recently gotten it to sell in his store. He said the arrowhead was made of metal and looked new, so that might help too. According to him, you will probably have a few really bad weeks but will probably live."

"Well, I'm glad about me," I said. "But I feel really awful about Alejandro and Jose. And I feel terrible for their families."

"Yes, me too," said all the guys at the same time.

When Carlos heard I was awake, he came over to talk to me about my wounds and what he had done. He said, "Bill, I would ask you how you're doing, but I know how you're doing, terrible! And believe me, you are going to feel worse. I am hopeful that you will be back to normal eventually. It will take at least a few weeks before you will want to be up and around much. A similar thing happened to me one time and the infection almost killed me. I hope you will do much better than that. The arrow hit you several inches below your heart. It came at an angle and proceeded down your left side raking your ribs, muscle, and skin. It finally stopped when it hit some thick muscle down by your belt."

"Wow," I said. "What did you do to clean the wound and patch me up?"

Carlos said, "That metal arrow sliced your side open pretty good which I think might be to your benefit. I could get into it and clean it better. When I got hit like that with an arrow, the wound couldn't be cleaned well enough. That's why the infection was so bad. I brought a jug of a new chemical called hydrogen peroxide with me. It is especially good at cleaning wounds. I used a lot of it on you. Hopefully, that will make a big difference on your wound and how it heals. And I used some ointment on the wound that should also make a difference on how it heals. I bound your wounds up with some clean cloth except the deeper wound where the arrowhead came to a stop. I took some thread and a needle and sewed some stitches there to hold you together better. I cleaned the area as good as I could, so hopefully you won't have a problem there. I'll check on it every day for a while to make sure it is looking alright. But for now, you should try not to move around much, so that it will all start to heal. I don't have anything to prevent the pain you will experience. I brought you a bottle of whiskey that should help some. I recommend you sip on it when you start to have serious pain."

"Thanks Carlos," I said. "I really appreciate you taking care of me. I'll try to take it as easy as I can."

Then Carlos said, "For now I would suggest you try to get as much sleep as you can. The more the pain sets in the more difficult it will be to sleep."

"I will," I said. I must have gone to sleep almost before he walked away.

When I woke up the next morning my chest felt like someone had sawed me in half. To say I felt terrible was not even close to how bad I really felt. Then I thought about Alejandro and Jose and their families. It was thrilling to be alive. I would try to remember that in the coming weeks as my body worked hard and painfully to heal.

I couldn't help but think that our caravan was lucky to have as many men as it did. I think the braves attacked our small group, just like a pack of wolves would attack any stragglers from a group of deer or antelope but wouldn't attack the larger group directly. We needed to make sure we didn't leave any of our group behind and it didn't matter for how long. The braves that attacked us saw a momentary opportunity and tried to take advantage of it. Thank God it didn't work quiet the way they wanted it to this time. We would need to be much more careful in the future.

Juan and Pablo decided that we needed to increase our guards at night from one to maybe three. Also, we needed to camp in areas that were as clear of trees and brush as we could. They didn't want it to be possible for any individual or group to sneak into our camp or even up close to it. The caravan was in a good position now. We would wait here until the five men that went to Albuquerque with the bodies of Jose and Alejandro had returned. It would likely be four to five days.

Juan had been riding Red around the area to look for signs of trouble. He stopped by to see me when he returned. "Bill, how are you feeling today? I left before you woke up this morning. I was thinking you would probably feel really bad when you did woke up."

I almost chuckled but it hurt too much. I said, "Juan, at first I really felt bad, but then I thought about Jose and Alejandro and decided I should just grit my teeth and thank God I'm still alive."

"Well, I'm sure glad you are still alive," Juan said. "We do need to count our blessings every day when we are on this trail."

I held up the bottle of whiskey Carlos had given me and said, "I have been medicating a little this morning and it does help. Carlos is going to stop by to see me after a while to see how I'm doing. The whiskey was his idea. In fact, he gave it to me. And I figured that any guy that could patch me up the way he did, should be listened to."

Juan chuckled and said, "Yes, I would certainly listen to him. He does know a lot about patching a person or animal up. He was in the Spanish Army for several years and doctoring was his main job. He learned a lot. I don't know that he is as good as a doctor, but you can sure trust him with most things."

I said, "Carlos told me that he got an arrow in the chest and almost died. Was that while he was in the army?"

"Yes, it was," Juan responded. "It is a wonder he lived. He was apparently in one of their field hospitals for a week or two and then was transported to a bigger facility where he stayed another couple of weeks. After he got well, the Army had him work in the hospital for almost a year. Even after Carlos's wounds healed, he was still disabled enough that the Army agreed to release him from any further duty. That's when he came back to Santa Fe and decided to make his living as a merchant."

"He learned a lot in that hospital about medicating and sewing up people. Before we got a doctor in Santa Fe, people were always going to Carlos for one thing or the other. Some days he could barely run his store for his doctoring."

"Well, I'm certainly glad he is with us on this trip," I said. "How did the countryside look as you were out riding around?"

"Great," Juan said. "I didn't see a thing."

Carlos stopped by about that time. He said, "Good morning Bill. How are you feeling?"

"I feel like a giant chewed me in half and then spit me out."

"Sounds like you need another swig of that medicine I left with you," Carlos said. "Why don't you open your shirt and lay back so I can look at your wounds."

I did what he told me to do and he had a look.

He said, "Bill, everything is still looking good. It is good that we are staying in one place for several days. Since we won't be riding in billowing dust, your wounds should get a good start at healing. But let me warn you again, there will be lots of pain and the harder you work at keeping the pain under control the better off you will be. So, don't hesitate to take a small mouthful of that whiskey when you feel you need to."

Before Carlos left, his brother Sid stopped by to see me. Then there was Leon and Manuel and Alberto. Of course, they were wanting to know how I was feeling. I assured them I wasn't feeling as bad yet as Carlos told me I would be feeling soon. We had a good time visiting. They all had a joke or two about me needing to be more careful. I would have enjoyed them more if laughing had not made my chest scream with pain. I was pretty sure that Carlos knew what he meant when it came to pain. I did want to take it seriously and get the healing started fast. So, I didn't move any more than I had to. And I quit listening to the jokes.

Over the next several days, all the men in the caravan stopped by to see me several times each. It was good of them to check on how I was doing. The Indian attack with the death of two of our friends and my injury seemed to draw all of us together even closer than we already were.

Juan and Pablo had been taking turns riding a wide perimeter around our camp to check for signs of possible problems. And the night guard with three men at a time was apparently going well. I was sorry that I didn't feel well enough to help them.

The weather had been warm and calm almost since the start of our trip. I certainly expected more in the way of winter cold and more snow; but we weren't seeing it. That was fine with me. I was staying warm in my bedroll by the fire most of the time. I had gotten up a couple of times when it was a necessity.

The pain in my chest had gotten much worse after a couple of days like Carlos said it would. I did my best to keep the pain away without rendering myself unconscious. However, that was unavoidable a few times.

By the evening of the fifth day, our other five men returned. They had been pushing hard and were really tired. Juan and Pablo thought we should give them a day of rest before the caravan started again.

The men told their stories about delivering the bodies to the families and the anguish they all, families and our men, felt. A Mass was held for each man as soon as possible and the bodies were buried.

Our men stayed long enough to tell the families about the Indian attack and to express their condolences. Then they headed back to us.

After giving our five men a day of rest, we got underway toward Chihuahua. It seemed like it had been a long time since we were on the road. I was still in my bedroll and riding in the back of the wagon. Luis was driving the wagon. I was hoping that in a day or two more I would feel like riding while sitting up. I was doing my best to keep the dust off my bandages.

By mid-day we were almost to La Joya, so it was decided to push on to Socorro to spend the night. We would stop at La Joya just long enough to fill our water barrels and then move on.

It was a difficult afternoon for me. My chest hurt like crazy. While we were filling our water barrels at La Joya, Carlos came and checked on my wounds. He changed some of the bandages and used some more ointment. Hopefully it would keep the wounds from getting any worse and help it heal. But unfortunately, it did nothing to relieve the pain. I did drink just a little whiskey. I didn't want to be light- headed if we happened to get attacked again. Of course, that seemed unlikely; but it was always a good idea to be ready for anything.

Laying in the back of the wagon, I could feel every slight bump in the road. I got to thinking that it might feel better to sit up, so the next time we took a break I rearranged my bedroll to put myself in a more upright position. It actually felt better. I rode the rest of the day that way. It wasn't great, but it was better than laying down. Tomorrow I thought I might try sitting up all day. If that worked alright, I might try sitting up and driving one of the wagons.

That evening as we camped at Socorro, the pain came back with a vengeance. It really hurt worse than it ever had. Carlos looked at the wounds and found an area where infection had set in. He cleaned that area with more hydrogen peroxide and then put on more ointment and a new dressing. I medicated myself with some more whiskey and went to sleep early. I didn't sleep well; but I did sleep.

The next morning, I felt bad enough that I gave up on my idea to sit up in the wagon. I just laid down in the wagon and tried to sleep, as Luis continued to drive. I slept most of the day, except when we were on really rough areas of the trail. I had bad dreams though. I dreamed about the Indian attack and about being alone in the wilderness. I even dreamed about being attacked by a gray wolf. It was a rough day. We finally got to a smooth part of the trail, and I slept well for what I supposed was several hours.

The next day was the same, with me sleeping in the bed of the wagon. But the day after that, I decided to try sitting up and actually driving the wagon. That worked well for a part of the day. Eventually, I went back to my bedroll in the bed of the wagon.

I felt amazingly better the next day and decided to drive the wagon again. I hoped to do it again the next day. It was nice to feel like I was doing something productive.

Carlos came to see me, as usual, just before supper. He said, "Bill, how was your day and how was the pain? I saw that you drove a wagon all day. How was that?"

I said, "Carlos, it wasn't too bad. I had pain, but it was bearable. It hurt severely a couple of times when I hit large bumps. But other than that, it was a decent day."

"Great! Let me take a look at your chest and see if you need some more ointment or fresh bandages."

Carlos looked at my wounds and the dressing. He said, "Bill, your wounds are all looking good. We need to keep watching them. They are all healing well and I don't see any infection."

I said, "Carlos, I am thinking about riding my horse tomorrow, unless you think that would be a bad idea. It seems to me that being more upright on my horse would be a smoother ride than bouncing along on the wagon. But, of course, if it doesn't feel good, I will give it up and go back to the wagon."

"I think that might be a good idea," Carlos said. "But try to take it easy and stop if the wounds start to hurt more."

"I will, Carlos," I promised.

The caravan started early the next day and I decided to start out driving the wagon. By mid-morning, that was getting uncomfortable, and I decided I would give riding Morgan a try. I asked Juan to take over driving the wagon. He did and I saddled up Morgan, with Luis' help.

I took over some scouting duties. One of Pablo's men was scouting to the east, so I rode to the west, but only a short distance. While it wasn't a cure for the pain, I did feel better. And I felt more useful to the whole caravan by scouting rather than driving our wagon. I probably didn't ride as much as I would have on a normal day, but I felt good about what I was able to do.

Carlos checked my wounds that evening and felt they were doing fine. He said as long as I was careful, I could probably do anything I wanted to do.

It was a quiet night, thank goodness. We probably were a little slower getting away in the morning than normal. We intended to ride a long day to put more miles behind us.

I told Juan I would like to ride scout again. I felt better on Morgan than on the wagon. That was fine with Juan so I started off early to get familiar with the area. I first rode behind the caravan about four or five hundred yards to see if I could see sign of anybody following us. I didn't see anything, so I rode back closer to the caravan. I did another circle round the caravan and then rode out front about five hundred yards.

I actually felt a little better today. I hoped it would last. If I continued to feel better for the next couple of days it would be another sign that the wounds were healing well. That would certainly be good.

The morning went well. Our trail at this point was fairly

wide and smooth. I had been looking for dust that might have been kicked up by any other group on either side of the river. I didn't see anything that bothered me.

There was a stop for a noon time break. The water barrels were filled while everyone was feeding and watering their animals. After a short rest, we drove on. I continued my riding at a distance from the wagons always staying more or less opposite the other scout as we circled the caravan. The weather had continued to be cold, but not uncomfortable. It should get warmer as we traveled farther south.

We made good time. The caravan got to the area of the hot springs about time to make camp. Again, we found a wide-open spot to stop for the night, so it would be less likely that anybody could try to sneak up on us.

The hot springs were known by everybody except me. Apparently, the springs had no official name; but was called Ojo Caliente, or hot eye in English, by several of the men in our group. They all chose not to visit it because it was a short ride down a dangerous trail to the west. I was certainly tempted because of my injury; but I stayed put with the caravan. Any relief I might find from the hot water would be outweighed by the possible danger.

All the animals were fed and watered especially well this evening. Tomorrow we would start into a long section of desert basin usually referred to as Jornada del Muerto or Journey of the Dead Man. For about three long days, we would be separated from the river and access to water. There would be two mountain ranges between the river and the caravan. They are Fra Cristobal and Caballo Mountains. We had planned for this occasion by bringing extra water barrels and food for the animals. Along the way we had taken advantage of all the grass we found for the animals to save the feed we brought with us. Hopefully we should still have plenty.

10 | JORNADA DEL MUERTO AND THE CHIHUAHUAN DESERT

Everyone was up early in the morning to start our trip. If it was June instead of December, and hot weather was going to be a problem, we would be traveling at night and resting in the heat of the day. But since that was not a problem now, everyone was ready to go at first light.

I was riding scout again. It really seemed to be helping my wound. I felt I was healing well. Carlos kept an eye on my wounds and I did some mild stretching when I could. However, I would admit that my chest ached something fierce at times. But I didn't think it was an infection. I thought it was just muscles trying to heal and I was certainly happy about that.

As the caravan took off, I was in the lead by maybe five hundred yards to see what was ahead of us. We all knew it would be desert sand for the next three, maybe four days. There wouldn't be any trees or shady areas. Again, it was thankfully December, so the heat was not a problem. We should be able to make good time. The route I found promised to be easy going for the caravan.

It was beautiful in a rough way. As we drove through the

desert there were mountains on both sides. The mountains were mostly bare and covered with rocks. There were some sparsely scattered trees and shrubs. Our trail was mainly sand with scattered small shrubs and cactus.

After I kept up the lead for a while, I finally faded back to the rear of the caravan for a time. I wanted to see if there was any evidence of anyone following us. There was not, so far as I could see. I rode in the rear for an hour and then went out to the east. Later, I rode to the west for a while. On the west we were separated from the river by mountains. It was unfortunate that we couldn't continue by the river; but that was too difficult and our current route was shorter.

The caravan stopped as evening was coming on us, so that all the animals could be fed and watered. We set up the guard rotation and everyone bedded down. It would be another long day tomorrow.

Two of Pablo's men, Javier and Alonso, were out looking for firewood when they ran into a group of rattlesnakes. They said there must have been six or seven of them. They appeared to be sunning themselves. This was the first time we had seen any snakes on our journey. The weather was getting warmer as we traveled south. We certainly would not have expected rattlesnakes in January. However, it was an especially warm day.

Javier and Alonso had found the snakes close to a large rock outcropping about two hundred yards from the camp. They left them there undisturbed. We felt it was unlikely they would be moving around, so they would not be a threat to our camp. It was good to know that they were around in case any of us wanted to go walking.

The next day was much like the previous one. I led out as scout and then circled back and took up my position in the rear. Then I moved to the east and later to the west. I became concerned about some dust I saw coming over the hills to our west. I watched that for about an hour and finally decided it was just wind picking up dust into the air. After all, it was a windy day and there was plenty of dust on our side of the hills also. Other than that brief concern, I found no evidence of anyone following us. We rode a long day and then camped for the night. Tomorrow night we should be on the southern edge of the Jornada del Muerto, if everything continued to go smoothly.

I had lost track of time since the attack by the Indian braves. I was in so much pain for the first week that I barely knew what I was doing part of the time. Gradually the pain got more bearable, and after ten days or so, I tried riding as a scout. That had gone fairly well. Then I drove the wagon, which also went well. Now we were almost three weeks past the attack. I still had pain; but it was much less than at first.

After the watch had been set up for the evening, Juan and I talked for a time before we settled down for the night. I asked, "Juan, how does this caravan compare to other ones you have gone on?"

"Most of them," he started, "have been a lot like this. We have been attacked by Indians before. I would have to say though that they usually are peaceful. The young braves like those that attacked us are sometimes just out to see how brave they can be or to settle some kind of score. They seem to be offended that people are crossing what they consider their land. I can't say that I blame them for that. They are nomadic and feel like all the country they roam is theirs. So, anybody who is anywhere near them is on their land. They especially don't like people on what they consider their hunting grounds.

"That Indian attack was unusual in that it seemed to be unplanned. They just saw our small group of wagons and made a reckless decision to attack you. I don't expect that we will see them again. That battle turned out much worse for them than they could have ever expected. I really feel sort of sorry for them. But I'm not the one that got an arrow in the chest. How are you feeling?"

"My chest is plenty sore," I answered. "But I don't think there is any infection, so I am doing alright. You know, I would feel a little sorry for those braves too, if they hadn't put an arrow in me and killed Alejandro and Jose. Do you expect we will have any more trouble either on the rest of this trip or on the way back to Santa Fe?"

"I doubt that we will have any further trouble on our trip to Chihuahua," Juan said. "I like what we have done about the triple watch at night and camping in areas where we can keep a good look out. And even though the country between here and Chihuahua is Apache country, I would be surprised if we had any further trouble. We haven't had any trouble from here on south before.

"Whether we will have any problems on the way back to Santa Fe is the question. I really doubt that we will. I'd say the group that attacked us was probably acting on their own volition. I doubt that they are going to want to drag any of their tribe into attacking us for revenge. It's possible that they would, but I would certainly be surprised. They probably got in serious difficulty when they got back to the tribe."

"That's great news as far as I'm concerned. I don't really want to see them again anytime soon," I said. "With that maybe I'd better settle down for the night and give these ribs some rest. I'll see you in the morning, Juan."

"Sleep well Bill," Juan said as we walked back to our bed-rolls.

The next morning, as usual, we were up and on the trail by first light. The trail continued to go smoothly and rapidly. I drove the wagon for the first time since I had started scouting to ease the pain on my ribs. It went well. The wound on my side was almost healed. Carlos was taking good care of me.

There was a quick stop around noon to water and feed the animals. Then we were on our way again. The caravan was making good time and we all hoped to be out of Jornada del

Muerto by time to camp for the night.

The afternoon continued well and by late afternoon we had gotten to the southern edge of our dangerous desert journey. Our route joined up again with the river and we were able to fill our water barrels and graze the animals on some good grass. Camp was made there for the night since it was an open area and fairly safe.

It was good to be out of the desert. We knew we had enough food and water to get through; but still, there is something about deserts that makes you feel trapped and fearful.

The next morning, we all got up a little slower, but still started in good time. Shortly after our noon stop, the caravan went by the village of Las Cruces. There was no reason to stop there, so the caravan kept on moving.

Juan and I were both riding as scouts this day. As we went near Las Cruces, we just happened to be riding near each other. Juan hollered over at me, "I can remember when Las Cruces was just a few houses. Now it looks like it is turning into a village. We used to have family that lived there. They moved to Albuquerque and settled down there. Our family would stop and see them when we were on the road to Chihuahua. Now there isn't much reason to stop there. However, if the village keeps growing, we may have to stop there someday."

As evening approached, we found a good place to camp. Our trip was starting to feel like it would soon be over, even though we had a big obstacle in front of us. We were already in the Chihuahuan Desert and would be in it the rest of the way to Chihuahua. Tomorrow afternoon we would get to El Paso. There we would lose the river and be going cross-country again. The river travels on to the southeast, but our trail will go almost directly south.

The next day was short. We reached the crossing of the river after we had been on the trail only a few hours. The crossing was not difficult because the river was low. I am sure there are times when crossing the river would be impossible. For our entire trip, we had been on the east side of the river. Now we crossed over to the west side. We would parallel the river for the rest of the day until we got to El Paso.

By early afternoon we were at El Paso del Norte. We would spend the rest of the afternoon filling water barrels and greasing wheels on the wagons and just generally getting ready for the last long leg of our trip. This part of our journey would take about eight more days, if everything went well. Even though we would not have the river for water anymore, we would have several places that we could stop for water.

After the animals were watered and fed for the evening, most of us took turns going into El Paso. Some had friends there and others just wanted to see the village. El Paso was a growing community on both sides of the Rio Grande. The location made me think that it would be an important city in the future.

Everyone was back early and we settled in for the night. We had relaxed our night watch to only two men per shift. Everyone thought that for this leg of the trip, the danger was passed. I hoped that was right. Juan felt that way and I couldn't see any reason not to agree.

The next morning everyone got up early and double checked the animal feed and water barrels. We all felt some momentum for Chihuahua. There was still over two hundred miles to go and we all hoped it would pass quickly.

I was riding as scout again. Morgan and I had a good day. The Chihuahuan Desert is much different than the sandy desert of Jornada del Muerto. This desert is rough and covered in plants. There was a large variety of cactus, yuccas, agave, mesquite, ocotillo and many other desert loving plants. These plants obviously didn't take much water because the climate in the desert is unusually dry. Thank goodness we were following an established trail. It would have been rough breaking a new one.

Even an established path didn't help in what came next. We

found huge sand hills that our mules crossed under the load of the wagons with much difficulty. We struggled for the entire day going through the deep sand and finally exited the sand hills before we found camp for the night.

The next day we carried on as normal through the rough desert. However, in the mid-afternoon, we got to a natural lake called Laguna de los Patos. The water was drinkable, though it had a mineral taste to it. The animals drank it but didn't seem to like it that well. We had enough water in our barrels that we decided to not fill them with this water and waited for fresher water down the trail.

A day later we reached the village of Carrizal. It appeared they were building a military fort there for troops to protect the local people from the ravages of the Apaches. We camped near there for the night.

In the morning we headed out with the intention of stopping at Ojo Caliente. This was a warm spring that apparently was well known and available year-round.

About mid-afternoon the caravan stopped at the springs and everybody had to try it out. I admit that I felt refreshed after taking an easy dip in the springs. The area of the springs was protected well enough that it was usable in about any kind of weather.

The caravan moved on after everyone had their opportunity in the springs. We camped several miles farther south. As we had grown accustomed to doing, we set out two man watches for the night after the animals were fed and watered. We found no grass in this area, so the animals ate hay that had been brought with us. Juan and I had been trading off as scout for the past few days. We had seen nothing that worried us. Andres, who was the scout from Pablo's group, had not seen any problems either.

Everyone had gotten up earlier than usual the next morning. The excitement of nearing Chihuahua was getting stronger each day. When the caravan moved out to the south, I rode Morgan to the north about a half mile to see if anything was following us. I couldn't see any kind of a threat, so I rode east and then circled around the entire caravan to end up on the western side. It still looked clear. By late afternoon the caravan started into the beautiful Encinillas Valley. There was an especially lovely lake near where we camped for the night. The water in the lake was fresh, so all the water barrels were filled. There was grass to feed the animals.

After all the chores were done with the animals, everyone congregated around one good-sized campfire. There was lots of general conversation about the day, which turned into talk about the entire trip. We mentioned what we had enjoyed and not enjoyed. The only time any of us was scared was the day of the Indian attack. Nobody particularly liked the Jornada del Muerto or the sand hills. But nobody expressed any dread at retracing our steps through there on the way back to Santa Fe. Most of us were concerned about returning through the area where the attack had taken place. But we all felt that following the procedures we had been using since the attack would keep us safe.

Juan moved the conversation to the past by telling stories about trips when he was younger. The road seemed to be safer then and whole families often made the trip. It is generally men only now. They all wanted to leave their families at home and look forward to bringing their families again someday when the road is safer.

Juan said, "I loved going to Chihuahua with our whole family. We still have family in Chihuahua and everybody would get together at the cathedral and on the square. We have a couple of cousins that were going to be priests and they were working at the cathedral. There was lots of food and drinking and dancing. We also played many games when we were young. We played tug of war, spinning tops, mublety-peg, horseshoes, hide and seek and tag. Then, before we left, there was a mass at the cathedral, a blessing for our return trip, and another meal. As I recall it took about thirty days each way, but it was worth it. We had a grand time."

Others joined in with their favorite trips and what their favorite things to do were. Some added what their intentions were once we got to Chihuahua. Most men were businessmen and came on the trip for the double purpose of selling what they brought with them and buying things to take back to Santa Fe. Everyone was anxious to get to Chihuahua.

11 | CHIHUAHUA

Everyone was up early in the morning and quickly got their equipment and animals ready to go. The excitement was still fairly blowing through the group like a breeze. We hoped to be in Chihuahua by mid-afternoon. Juan was riding on Red as one of the scouts and I was driving the wagon. Louis and Lorenzo had been on the other wagon together for most of the way. They didn't seem to know what to think about getting to Chihuahua. They had never been anywhere except for Santa Fe. They had seemed unusually quiet the past few days.

By mid-day we could practically feel how close we were getting to Chihuahua. It wouldn't be long until we could start to see it in the distance. First, we would be able to see the spires on the cathedral and then gradually the rest of the town.

All in all, it was a cloud of dust that we saw in the distance that signaled we were nearing Chihuahua. It was a still day and the dust from the caravan just hung suspended in the air. So, another cloud of dust in the distance signaled to us that we were nearing Chihuahua.

We soon saw the double spires of the cathedral. They were

impressive even from a distance. It didn't take long until we were beginning to see homes on the outskirts of town. Many of them were made of adobe, some were made of native stone. Most houses had animals penned up out back. There were a lot of sheep, some milk cows, the occasional beef calf, or cow, and almost every home had a dog and chickens. Some homes had pigs.

Many people stopped what they were doing and waved at our group as we rolled into town. They were friendly and welcoming; but I didn't expect any less. After a little while our caravan got to the center of town and circled the square. On one side was the Metropolitan Cathedral of the Holy Cross, Our Lady of Regla, and St. Francis of Assisi. What looked impressive from a distance looked magnificent from this close. The cathedral was partially adobe, partially native stone, and dark brick. It was a beautiful combination. Much of the plaza was also dark brick. What wasn't brick was grass. It was larger than the plaza in Santa Fe.

We were guessing that some family members might have heard of our caravan coming toward Chihuahua. We didn't know there would be such a large group to welcome us. Apparently, they had been keeping track of our caravan for the last few days by locals that had been out in the country visiting friends.

Most of the men in our caravan had someone there to greet them. Some of them, like Juan, had an entire group at the square. It was quite a gathering. Everyone was excited and shaking hands and hugging. There were individuals and groups. Priests and nuns from the cathedral were family to some of our group.

Even some local businesspeople were on the square. It was not clear if they were among the friends and family group or if they just wanted to see what our caravan had brought to their fair city.

It did appear that later we would be having a meal together in celebration of our arrival. Several people looked to be opening roasting pits that had been covered with dirt for many hours to hold in the heat. The aroma of the cooked meat was unbelievable. There were tables and benches already set up in the square. It also appeared there was going to be music during or after the meal. I saw several men with stringed instruments sitting up to play.

Juan came up about that time to introduce me to a group of people, "Bill, I want you to meet some of my family. This is my Aunt Anita and my Uncle Claudio. And these are their lovely daughters Josepha and Frances. They also have a son Ronaldo who is studying at the cathedral."

Before Juan could say anymore, they all hugged me and said, "Welcome to the family Bill." Juan had apparently told them all about me already. It was great to be welcomed with such warmth. I almost cried. It was obvious they were Juan's family. Not only did they look like his relatives back in Santa Fe, but they had similar personalities to his family.

I said, "It is wonderful to meet you all and I am glad and honored to be welcomed into your family. Juan and his family back in Santa Fe have been so nice to me and are such wonderful people. I can't imagine a family I would rather be part of. Thank you for your welcome."

Juan wasn't exaggerating when he called the girls lovely. They truly were. Frances, the oldest, was tall and elegant with flowing black hair, sparkling brown eyes and a perpetual smile. Her younger sister, Josepha, was almost as tall and slender as Frances. She also had beautiful black hair and brown eyes.

Anita and Claudio were both tall and made a handsome couple. Claudio had silver hair and was probably six feet three inches tall. Anita had dark hair with a touch of gray. She looked like a slightly older version of her daughters.

Juan continued, "They live west of Chihuahua several miles. They raise fruit as well as sheep and goats and a few beef cattle. They also have a store here in town where they sell tools, rope, leather, lumber, weapons and other household and farm items. They have a house in town as well as one on the rancho."

Juan turned as somebody else walked up to us. He said, "Bill, here is their son Ronaldo."

Ronaldo walked up with Luis and Lorenzo. He appeared to be several years older than them. The plain black cassock he was wearing showed that he was studying at the cathedral. And while his height wasn't quite that of his father's, it was close.

"Ronaldo, I want you to meet my friend Bill Rampy. His brother Troy is a good friend of mine from my sailing days. Bill came to see me and has been helping me in my trading post."

Ronaldo stuck out his hand and said, "Hi Bill. It is a pleasure to meet you. Welcome to Chihuahua. Oh, Luis and Lorenzo were telling me you got an arrow in your chest on the trip down to Chihuahua. God must have had his angels watching over you."

"Yes, He sure did," I responded. "The arrow hit me just right or I might not have made it here."

"Well, I am certainly glad it hit you right," Ronaldo responded. "Praise be to God."

I said, "Thank you. It is a pleasure to meet you."

And with that someone suggested that the meal was about ready to begin.

The crowd was moving toward some tables that held the food. It consisted of slow barbecued young goat and lamb as the main course. There were yams and another root vegetable that I was not familiar with. There were piles of freshly made tortillas and jugs of water. The crowd slowly went through the line and got what they wanted. They clearly were more interested in visiting with their friends and relatives than eating. I was pretty interested in eating because the aroma rising from the food was rich, warm, and spicy.

When I got my food, I sat down close to Juan and his family. They were unusually excited to see each other, and their food was disappearing about as fast as mine. The lamb was especially good. I had eaten lamb before and liked it. The goat was even better. I had never had it before and was surprised how good it was. It tasted like beef; but was as tender as chicken. It really did almost melt in my mouth. And everything else was tasty also.

Juan got my attention and said, "Bill, move over here a little closer and tell my family where you are from and how you got here. I was telling them some of your history. You obviously can tell your story better," he laughed.

I started off at the beginning, "I grew up in eastern Alabama which is a U.S. state along the Gulf Coast and north of the western part of Florida. I grew up in a large family. There were four boys and four girls. My oldest brother is named Troy. He is the one that left home early and decided to start sailing along the east coast of the United States. He met Juan who was also sailing at that time. They became good friends after they worked side by side on a couple of ships. When they parted, Juan went back to Santa Fe and Troy went to New Orleans. In New Orleans, Troy became a merchant selling a little bit of everything. After a few years he had become a good businessman."

Juan interrupted and said, "Troy was about the nicest person I have ever known. His word was his bond. If he told you he would do something, he would do it. I would love to see him again. We had our big families in common, but there was much more than that. We just seemed to think alike. I could tell Bill was his brother when I first met him. He is just like his brother Troy. It has been a pleasure working with Bill, just like working with Troy. I don't say all this to flatter Bill or his brother. I just want you to know the character of men they are. I'm sorry to interrupt, Bill. Please go ahead with your story."

"Juan, I'm not sure what to say now with a comment like that, but thank you," I continued. "My brother has told me stories about you and the character of man you are. He always referred to you as a special person. And that is what I have thought of you since I have been here." I took another drink of water and then went on with my story. "I wanted to travel, so I eventually traveled to New Orleans to see Troy. I worked a while with him and enjoyed the trading business. We both had an interest in trading in the west. We had heard that Santa Fe would be a good market. We thought that once the war between Mexico and Spain was over, Santa Fe would be in need of new trading partners. Troy and I thought that I should travel to Santa Fe. We thought I should spend enough time there to see what might be needed in the way of dry goods."

"I saddled up a good horse and packed up two more and headed across country from New Orleans to Santa Fe. I traveled up the Mississippi River and then west along the Atchafalaya River until I got to the Red River. I paralleled the Red River for several hundred miles. Then I went across country until I got to the Pecos River and eventually to Santa Fe. I lost my two pack horses and all my trade goods along the way; but other than that, I made it to Santa Fe safely. I met Alphonse and Christine in Santa Fe and they told me where to find Juan. We have been having a great time together. So that is pretty much my story."

Juan said, "Bill, you didn't say anything to them about the arrow in your chest. I told them about the attack, so you can skip that part."

I laughed a little nervously and said, "Well, I was unusually lucky. The arrow hit my ribs in a glancing blow and finally stopped low on my side. Carlos Poso, one of the merchants with us, cleaned up the wounds good and put some ointment on them and kept them bandaged, so they wouldn't get infected. He did a great job! I felt bad for several weeks. I am doing much better now. He said the arrow had a medal tip that cut most of my side open before stopping in some thicker flesh down low on my side. Because I was cut open, it made my side easier for Carlos to clean. After he got me cleaned up good, he took needle and thread to sew me up in some of the worst places. I feel lucky that Carlos was with us. God certainly had his angels looking after me."

I noticed that Josepha and Frances were looking at me with their eyes wide and their mouths open in surprise. They were both lovely girls.

After an hour or so of visiting, eating, and more visiting, music began to get everyone's attention. All the food was cleaned up quickly and people began to gather around the music. There were several guitars, a violin, and a bass guitar. The group played easily. It sounded like they had lots of practice together. Many in the crowd started to dance. Other people from town started to filter into the plaza when the music started.

Juan's aunt and uncle started to dance. They were especially smooth and fluid. Then Juan found an old friend and they began to dance. Several in our group had moved out to join the rest as they danced. I wasn't considering it because I had only danced that once in Santa Fe. I walked over to the side to get out of the way of the dancers.

Frances walked up to me and said, "Bill, would you like to dance?"

She was in a long skirt with a white blouse and a green vest. Her black hair went about halfway down her back and was silky and especially beautiful. I had never seen anybody so stunning.

"I have only danced once in my life," I said. "But I could not say no to a woman as beautiful as you."

She blushed and said, "Maybe I can teach you a little. I have been dancing ever since I was a little girl."

She held out her arms to me and we started to dance slowly. It was relatively easy because we were dancing one of the dances I had learned in Santa Fe. Her movements were smooth and graceful. She was about three inches shorter than me. I was guessing that she was probably six years younger than me. I was twenty-eight, so I was guessing her to be twenty-two.

"Have you lived here your whole life?" I asked.

"Yes, I have," she answered. "My family has lived here for several generations. They came here from Spain as settlers and have been here since then. Oh, we did have some of the family move to Santa Fe; but everybody else stayed in this area. Most of the family have been ranchers or merchants or both. We have had some of our family, like our brother, find a calling to the church. My sister has recently finished school locally. She is not sure what she will do next."

As we continued to dance and flow with the rest of the crowd, I said without really thinking about it, "What about you? Do you have a boyfriend?" I was embarrassed by my own question and said, "I'm sorry, I shouldn't have asked you such a personal question. Please forgive me."

She laughed and said, "That's alright. I don't have a boyfriend. I have been away in Mexico City going to school. When I was young all I ever wanted to be was a teacher. There is such a large need for teachers here, and every place, I guess. So, when I finished school here, I went off to the University and studied, so I could become a teacher. I came back to Chihuahua a few months ago and am now teaching in the school attached to the cathedral. I enjoy it a great deal."

"What do you teach?" I asked.

The music had changed, and we were dancing a different dance, and I was able to follow along.

"I teach a little bit of everything. I want to teach whatever is needed. My favorites are mathematics, science and geography. At the cathedral I teach everything except Bible."

"I understand that your brother is studying to be a priest at the cathedral. Has he been there a long time," I asked?

"He is nearly finished," she responded. "He should get a parish sometime this coming summer. He has always loved the church. He will be a wonderful priest. I hope that his parish will be close to Chihuahua or that he will come back to the cathedral someday soon."

The dance went on for several hours. Frances and I talked through the evening. She was easy to talk to and a good dancer. She made me feel like I could actually dance. We danced most of the evening. Part of the time we sat down and talked.

By the time the evening was over, I asked, "Could I see you again sometime?"

She laughed and said, "You'll have to. You, Juan, Louis, and Lorenzo are coming out to our rancho for supper tomorrow night."

"Great. I'll be looking forward to it," I said.

"Me too," Frances said.

With that, she went to catch her parents and I went to find Juan and the rest of our caravan.

Some of the group had moved the entire caravan around into an empty area and circled the wagons to let the animals loose, after feeding and watering them. Juan and I bedded down by our wagons. Luis and Lorenzo were spending the night with Ronaldo at the cathedral.

As I was laying there in my bedroll, I couldn't help but think what a magical night it had been for me. I had more than enjoyed my short time in Chihuahua. It was a special place with many fine people and families. The greeting we received, along with the supper and dance, were more than I ever expected. I really enjoyed meeting Juan's family. And I especially enjoyed talking and dancing with Frances. She was a wonderful woman and I loved getting to know her. With those thoughts in my head, I eased off to sleep. I had nothing but wonderful dreams.

The next morning, everybody in our caravan slept late. From here on, until we regrouped to go back to Santa Fe, the caravan was partially broken up. Everyone would be going their own way. Those with relatives and friends in Chihuahua would probably spend their day with them. Then tomorrow everyone with merchandise to sell or things they needed to buy, would start working on those details. However, the whole group from the caravan would still be sharing some guard duties.

Juan and I had several people we wanted to see before heading out to his aunt and uncle's rancho for supper. Luis, Lorenzo,
and Ronaldo would be going with us. They would be spending
the morning together and then meet up with Juan and me just in
time to go to the rancho.

Juan wanted to take me to a café near the square for breakfast. It was a place he always wanted to eat when he came to
Chihuahua as a kid. It was a white adobe building with wood
beams protruding from the corners similar to the governor's
palace in Santa Fe. It had a full porch across the front. There
was a warm and friendly atmosphere inside. Strings of drying
red chilis hung from the corners of each window. The room was
about thirty feet by twenty feet.

Juan and I ordered green chili pork with tortillas, beans, and
coffee. Juan insisted that we also have cake. He said it was the
best. He was right. It was warm, creamy, and delicious.

We ran into Carlos and Sid Poso there. They had just finished eating and were going to visit a couple of their friends in
town. Sid had an old friend here that he had studied with in law
school. Then Carlos wanted to visit with a couple of store owners that he knew well. They also had family in town they would
be seeing in the afternoon.

Carlos had checked my wounds the night before and felt they
were in good shape. There was one spot that he put some more
ointment and a clean bandage on. Other than that, he thought
everything else looked essentially healed. I was glad about that.
To know that my risk of serious infection was almost over was
exciting. With a wound like I had from the arrow, infection and
how quickly it could have killed me, was on my mind constantly
since the fight.

When we settled down to eat our breakfast, Juan asked,
"How are you enjoying Chihuahua, Bill? I have always enjoyed
visiting here, partly because the town is beautiful and partly

because of our relatives that live here."

I answered, "I like it a lot too and for the same reasons. The town, so far as I have seen, is neat and attractive. And I love your family too."

Juan responded, "I noticed last night that you seem to especially like my cousin Frances. And it seemed that she liked you in return. If you stay around here a long enough maybe you can become a part of my real family instead of just adopted family. I think I would like that, Bill." Juan laughed, and I'm sure I blushed, if someone as tanned as me could still blush.

"Well, maybe we should talk about something a little less embarrassing. Frances was probably just being nice to me last night," I said.

"Maybe," he said. "But you both seemed to have a special twinkle in your eyes last night."

"Juan," I said, "I think you are just seeing things."

The breakfast was delicious, especially the cake, and the atmosphere of the café was friendly and comfortable, even with the constant chatter of a large crowd. It had been here for many years and had gained more character with each year. The green chili pork and tortillas were especially tasty. They were easily the best I had ever had.

Our first stop was a blacksmith shop where we bumped into Manuel. He and Juan visited a little while with the owner, Mateo. Mateo used to be in Santa Fe and was the one that taught Manuel most of what he knew about blacksmithing. He moved to Chihuahua to be closer to his parents who were getting older.

Juan and I left Manuel with Mateo and walked down the street to a clothes store. It was being run by another old friend, Joseph, who had grown up in Santa Fe and then moved here a decade ago.

What I had seen so far of Chihuahua was clean and attractive. Most of the buildings and homes were either made of native stone or adobe. Some homes were made of wood, which was scarce in the local vicinity and had to be hauled in from quite a distance. Adobe bricks were made of mud and straw or other plant material, so that was a much more common building material. Roofs were generally flat with a slight slope to the back which allowed the occasional rain to drain off. Adobe was often left a natural brown or reddish-brown color; but sometimes painted white or tan.

Joseph had an attractive store with lots of men's clothes. There were both work clothes and clothes that were dressier for celebrations and church.

Juan and Joseph hugged each other as we walked into the store. Juan spoke first and said, "Joseph, how are you? It has been so long since I've seen you. You look like you have aged well and your store looks prosperous."

"Juan, I'm doing well. Thank you. But, how are you? The last I heard you were off sailing the world. What are you doing now?"

Joseph was a tall handsome man that dressed like a clothing merchant. He wore a dress shirt with a string tie. He also wore black slacks that looked as if they had been pressed with a hot iron. His hair was black with threads of silver.

Juan laughed and said, "I did sail a bit. I've been back in Santa Fe or the Santa Fe area for a while now. I run a trading post about halfway between Santa Fe and Taos. I really enjoy it. Oh, I tried trapping for a season and decided I wasn't skilled enough to do that for a living. Hey, speaking of sailing, I want you to meet the brother of a wonderful friend I made during my sailing days. Joseph, this is Bill Rampy. I met his brother, Troy, on a sailing ship. We worked side by side for a while and quickly became friends. Troy is in the dry goods business in New Orleans. Bill was working with him and they decided he should come to Santa Fe to investigate the possibility for selling merchandise to the merchants there. I brought him to Chihuahua as an extension of his research," he chuckled.

Joseph stuck out his hand and said, "Bill, it is nice to meet you. I've known Juan since we were acolytes together at the cathedral in Santa Fe. Juan said your brother was in the dry goods business in New Orleans. What kind of merchandise does he sell there?"

"He has a store there," I said. "He sells a wide variety of household and hardware items. He sells usually to people who are moving somewhere else as a settler or new people to the area that need to furnish their house with general supplies. He doesn't sell large items like furniture, but rather small items all the way from food to dishes, clothes, boots, tools and other equipment for raising gardens and orchards."

Joseph responded, "Juan said you came to Santa Fe to investigate selling dry goods there?"

"Yes, that's right. We can't help but think that when the war between Mexico and Spain is over, Santa Fe will be a good area for selling general merchandise. There are several large or growing U.S. cities that are not too far from Santa Fe. We can imagine that many businesspeople will want to bring wagons loaded with goods to sell to merchants there. I just came here to get a basic education in the area. Troy wanted me to find Juan just to get to know him. We had no idea that he had a trading post and so many friends in business. I have been able to get far more education than I anticipated and made many more friends."

Joseph said, "Let's go next door and we can have a little lunch. My clerk can take care of the store while I am gone."

Joseph let the clerk know we were going next door to eat. We walked next door and got a seat at a table by the front window and all ordered chili, bread, and coffee.

Juan said, "Joseph, it looks like you are doing well. You must enjoy it here in Chihuahua."

"I really do enjoy it here," said Joseph. "But I would have to admit that my store is only part of the enjoyment. I have a wife and four children now. That has added more to my life than I ever thought possible. Do you have a family, Juan?"

"No, I don't," Juan answered. "I intend to do that sometime. I just keep thinking I will do it next year. Next year comes and then I think, well maybe next year. But I do intend to find somebody to love one of these days. I don't want to live my entire life alone."

The chili came and we all dug into our bowls. It was really hot chili. I wasn't sure about the meat. I assumed it was lamb, but it could have been beef. It was certainly delicious; but almost too hot to eat. After we finished our chili, Juan and I decided we should move on. We said a warm goodbye to Joseph and headed down the street.

We spent a little more time just walking around town. Then Juan decided it was time to find the rest of our group for supper and head to the rancho.

12 | THE RANCHO

We found Luis and Lorenzo at the cathedral with Frances's brother, Ronaldo. Juan and I rode Red and Morgan to give them a little exercise. Luis and Lorenzo took two of the spare horses that we had kept tied at the back of the wagons. Ronaldo had his own horse that he kept stabled near the cathedral.

It was a beautiful ride of only a couple of miles west from Chihuahua to the rancho. We rode easily so as not to get too dusty on the way there. The road was well traveled and maintained, with a variety of native plants along the road. There were many grasses, several types of cacti, and a couple of different types of yuccas. In addition, there were several blooming plants which surprised me. I didn't realize we were far enough south to have flowers blooming in January.

When we got near the house, Ronaldo took Luis and Lorenzo toward the barns. Juan and I went to the front of the house.

The rancho headquarters consisted of a large adobe ranch house, two corrals, a large barn, three smaller barns, a garden, and an orchard. Juan told me that they also had several large pastures.

Three large dogs met us as we rode up to the house. They were friendly and practically invited us into the house. Their job must have been to alert the family to our arrival.

As we dismounted and walked up to the front porch, Josepha was the first to greet us. She hugged us both and said, "Papa is down at the barn doctoring one of the horses. Mama and Frances are upstairs dressing. They should be down soon. How was the ride out to the rancho?"

Josepha was the youngest child and probably more outgoing than her siblings. She was friendly and talked to us about the rancho and what she had been doing recently. She had finished school locally and was trying to decide what to do next. She looked amazingly like her mother but was several inches shorter. She was as stunning as Frances.

Juan said, "It was enjoyable with all the beautiful plants along the road. I have always loved this place. It is great to be here again."

I added, "It really is lovely here. Did you grow up on the Rancho or in town?"

"In between," she said with a laugh. "We have had both places all of my life. I think the house in town was purchased when Ronaldo was small. That gave Mama and Papa time to be with Ronaldo and be close to the business in town too. They have several employees that have always worked and lived on the rancho, so Mama and Papa don't need to be here all the time." She motioned to several chairs on the front porch and said, "Why don't you both have a seat and I'll get us something to drink."

About the time Josepha got back with glasses of water, Claudio returned from the barn. He greeted us warmly and said he would go wash up.

Juan asked, "Josepha, what are you going to do now that you have finished school here in Chihuahua? Will you go to school in Mexico City like Frances?"

"I don't know, Juan. I'm just not sure. Part of me wants to go to Mexico City and the other part of me wants to go to... oh, I just don't really know. Do you have any suggestions?"

Juan laughed, "No. I don't have any suggestions. I'm sure Mexico City would be wonderful. Or maybe you could go to Spain or the United States. You know that I got my advanced education sailing along the coast of the United States. But I wouldn't suggest that for a lady. Maybe going to school in Mexico City would be best. What does your heart tell you?"

"That's the hard part," she said. "I just don't know what I want to do or where I want to go."

"You could come back to Santa Fe with us," said Juan. "My parents would love to host you for as long as you would like to stay. It would get you away from Chihuahua for a time and maybe give you a different perspective."

"That would be fun," she said. "I love your parents. Living with them for a time in Santa Fe would be interesting. I'll think about that."

"What would your parents like for you to do?" Juan asked.

"I'm not sure about that either," she said. "I suppose they are open to different things. If I got called to the church, I'm sure they would be proud of me, just like they are proud of Ronaldo. But I have not felt a call to the church. And if I wanted to go to Mexico City, they would support me in that too. Going to Spain or the U.S. might be a little more difficult for them. Frankly, it might be a more difficult for me too. I would love to see the U.S. and Spain both someday, but I think I would be afraid to go that far away."

About that time Aunt Anita and Frances stepped out onto the porch. They hugged us both and asked us into the house for supper. Frances was wearing a long tan riding skirt with a light blue blouse. I had a hard time breathing when I looked at her.

Luis, Lorenzo, and Ronaldo must have come in the back door, because they were already sitting at the large, polished wood dinner table when we came in. It was large enough to hold about ten or twelve people. It had a beautiful lace runner down the middle from end to end. The chairs surrounding the table were all made of the same wood.

Supper was already laid out. The cook and housekeeper, Maria, had done a wonderful job. She was a small friendly woman that had been a part of the family since before Ronaldo was born. She had prepared a main course that was leg of lamb. There were also several vegetables that had been roasted with the lamb and yams. Two stacks of tortillas were arranged by the food.

Claudio asked Ronaldo to bless the meal. Ronaldo stood smiling and prayed over the meal. Then he prayed for our time together and asked for safety for our time in Chihuahua. With that, we all politely started passing around the food. There was not much conversation. Everyone enjoyed the meal and told Maria of their appreciation. The whole family loved her.

With not much said during the meal, we all retired to the living room for coffee and conversation. The large living room was filled with all of us there.

Ronaldo was the first to speak. He said he would like to say a short prayer and that he had an announcement. He stood again and then prayed a short prayer for family, friends, and the church. After the prayer, he said, "I have been talking to Luis and Lorenzo ever since they have been in Chihuahua. And I am proud that they have asked me to make an announcement on their behalf. I could not be happier to make this announcement for them. Both Luis and Lorenzo want you to know that they are feeling a call to the church. They say that this is something they both have been feeling for some time. They feel their visit to the cathedral here has confirmed that call in their hearts. Their intentions are to stay in Chihuahua and study here. I have talked to Bishop Garcia. He interviewed them both and has given them his blessing to stay at the cathedral and join us in study."

Juan spoke up and said, "Before we left Santa Fe, I talked to their mother, Isabella, and she told me they were feeling a call to the church. So, if we don't bring them home in the caravan, their family will not be surprised." He stood and said, "I am proud of you young men!" And with that he started clapping for them.

Everyone else rose and began clapping for them too. It was an exciting moment, although nobody was completely surprised. The Leos family, over the generations, had many of their sons and daughters called to the church to do God's work. Every time it happened there was always a large upwelling of joy in the family, because they all felt as if they were being called to God's work. Everyone was immensely proud this evening for Luis and Lorenzo.

Maria refreshed everyone's coffee and we continued talking about the church, life, and our families. We talked about our families' histories and our outlook for the future. We talked about the coming future of Mexico as it looked like it would soon separate itself from Spain. And even though Juan's family had come to Mexico from Spain many years ago, they felt themselves to be citizens of Mexico, and not Spain. They were ready for their country to move forward as an independent Mexico. It was an exciting evening, even for me. I felt more and more like part of their family.

As the conversation slowed somewhat, Frances asked if I would like her to show me around their rancho. I said of course, so we congratulated Luis and Lorenzo again, and then excused ourselves. We headed out the back door and walked toward the corral by the biggest barn. It was a large rock barn that had a hay loft in an upper level and was open under that, except for six or eight horse stalls on one side.

In the corral were six beautiful horses. I wasn't sure what breed they were at first, but they looked fast. They were obviously well cared for.

"They are Andalusians from Spain," Frances said as she

came up beside me. "My father has a friend in Madrid that sent him a stallion and a mare about ten years ago. We raise them now."

"They really are stunning. Are they as fast as they look?" I asked.

"They are fast," she said. "But speed is not the most important part of riding them. They hold their heads up in an erect position and they have a gait that is smoother than other horses. They are enjoyable to ride. Would you like to ride one?"

"Certainly, I would love to," I answered. I had heard of Andalusians before. It was amazing to finally see one. All I knew about them was that some people referred to the as the Pure Spanish Horse. Their ancestors had lived in Spain for thousands of years. And I knew that they had been recognized as a breed for several hundred years.

We walked through the barn into the corral. She clapped her hands, then whistled for the two horses to come to her. One was a silver-gray mare and the other was a dappled white stallion. She put bridles over their heads and tied each of them to the corral fence

"Come back in the barn with me and we will get saddles," Frances said. "The stallion belongs to Ronaldo; but he would be happy for you to ride it. He calls it The Wind. It stays out at the ranch and he rides another horse back and forth to town. I call my mare Sunshine."

We got two saddles out of the barn. They were similar to what I was used to; but they were lighter in weight. The leather in each of them was smooth and supple.

Frances started saddling Sunshine immediately. I started to saddle The Wind and was surprised at how tall he was. I don't know why I didn't realize that when I first saw him. He must be a hand higher than Morgan. Until now, I thought Morgan was a pretty tall horse.

"Give me a leg up, Bill," Frances said.

I helped her on to Sunshine and then I mounted The Wind a little less gracefully than I wanted to. The horses were attractive and stood with a gracefulness that I had never seen before. We walked them back through the barn. Then we trotted the horses easily toward the orchard. Once we were out in the clearing between the barn and the orchard, Frances slapped Sunshine easily across the neck with the reins. Sunshine seemed to be at full speed instantly. I did the same with The Wind and he took off so fast that I felt like I was going to blow off his back. I had never ridden a horse that fast. We had to slow down quickly or would have run right past the orchard. I thought I would like to try that again for a little longer run. If their stamina was as good as their acceleration, they were impressive animals.

When we stopped at the orchard, Frances and I got off the horses. Frances dropped the reins from Sunshine and she stood still. I dropped the reins on The Wind and he stood still also. The horses remained still and waited for us to pick up the reins again.

"My mother and father love our orchards," Frances said. "They are their special project. Our family raised fruit in Spain. Actually, we still have family in Spain that grow fruit trees as their business. My family originally cared for these orchards as a hobby. In recent years we have started selling some of what we raise because we can't eat it all."

"What do they grow?" I asked. "When I was young, we had a couple of apple trees and a cherry tree. My mother would make both apple and cherry pies. They were a special treat for the family. And that is the extent of my fruit tree knowledge."

Frances said, "They grow several different varieties of plums primarily. They also grow a wide variety of apples, and even some citrus fruit. The growing season is long here. If you are familiar with trees and how they grow, you can see that the buds are starting to swell now. They should start leafing out in about six weeks or so."

"I don't know a lot about trees," I said, "but it is easy to see that a great deal of care has been given to all of these trees. I would like to see them when they are leafed out and have fruit on them."

"I hope you will come back when they are in fruit," she said. "How long will you be in Santa Fe?"

"My intention is to leave for St. Louis when the weather warms up in the spring. I don't have a definite time," I said.

"Maybe you could come back to Chihuahua before you leave," she suggested.

"I would love to, but it is a long trip. I'm not sure I would have time."

"You have friends here now," she said with a smile as she moved closer to me. "Perhaps we should go back to the house. I think there are some empanadas and coffee for dessert."

We walked back to the horses. I had never seen horses that ground tied like these two. They had not moved a foot. We mounted up and took a short ride around the perimeter of their rancho headquarters. There was enough distance that we let the horses run again. This time they ran a lot longer. The Wind was appropriately named. He truly could run like the wind, as could Sunshine. When we got back to the barn, we let them both drink from a trough while we took off the saddles and brushed them down. They were striking and intelligent horses. It was a pleasure to ride them, and even more of a pleasure to be with Frances. She was certainly special.

We walked up to the house talking about the horses and what we both intended to do for the next few months. I could smell the empanadas as we walked back into the house. Everyone had gathered back around the table for dessert and a fresh round of coffee. They were talking about family and what we were doing the next few days. We got back just in time. The coffee and empanadas had just been brought to the table. Everyone was passing them around. They were pumpkin filled, which was appropriate for this time of the year. They had a warm earthy taste and were as good as I had ever eaten. The coffee was strong and dark. It even tasted good with a little added cream.

Juan asked, "Where have you two been?"

I said, "We were out riding around the orchards and seeing how fast The Wind and Sunshine can run. I have never seen horses like them before. I had heard of Andalusians but never seen one. They were amazing."

"I got to ride one once," Juan said, "but I had to beg them to ride it then. You're right; they are truly amazing."

Ronaldo said, "The Wind is the horse that I usually ride when I am here. I don't get to ride him much anymore. I'm glad you got to ride him. He does love to run. He was raised here at the rancho."

It was getting late by the time we had dessert, so we all were invited to spend the night at the rancho. We had intended to go back into town; but it had gotten dark and there was no moon. Maria got it sorted out where we could sleep. Ronaldo, Luis, and Lorenzo all slept in Ronaldo's room. There was a guest bedroom with two beds, so Juan and I slept there.

The next morning, I got up early and was going outside to see how the weather was. It was cool. I was wearing a light-weight brown jacket. Maria had already made coffee and offered me a cup, so I took it outside to the front porch. I sat in a swing tied by ropes to a beam in the ceiling of the porch.

"Can I join you?" Frances asked. She had just come out onto the porch.

"Certainly," I said nervously. I had just been thinking about her. It startled me when she came out onto the porch. She was wearing a riding outfit with a tan ankle length split skirt and a dark blue top. Frances looked as special as ever. "How are you?" I asked.

She sat down close to me on the swing. "I am good. Thank you. How are you?"

"I'm good," I said. "But I wish I didn't have to leave. It is wonderful here. And it is especially nice to get to know you better."

She smiled. "It is nice to get to know you better also. What will you and Juan do today?"

"There are other businesspeople in town that he wants to visit," I said. "The town should get much busier with more traders coming in this week. Juan has some items he wants to sell and other items he wants to buy to take back to his trading post. We should have fun. After all, the reason for my coming to Santa Fe in the first place was to learn about buying and selling dry goods in this part of the world. This week should teach me a lot. Just being around Juan has taught me far more than I anticipated. He is an intelligent businessman."

"Yes, he is," she said. "I have always enjoyed being around him. He is my cousin; but he is older, and almost seems like my uncle. He has done a lot of different things in his life. I enjoy hearing him talk about his days on a ship. I actually remember him telling stories about adventures he had with a friend. That must have been your brother."

Just then Maria came out onto the porch and gave us both large cinnamon buns that were fresh out of the oven. We thanked her and quickly ate them. They were slightly sweet and had an aroma of both cinnamon and something else I couldn't make out. Maybe it was nutmeg. They were delicious. The coffee even tasted better after the buns. Juan walked around the corner of the house about that time. He had been out to the small corral near the house where we had kept our horses overnight. He suggested that we go back to town soon.

I got up and told Frances that I hoped I would see her again soon. She had already gotten to her feet from the swing. She gave us both warm hugs and said she would see us in town. Her parents were going to need her help at their store during the fair, so she would be there most of the week.

Juan and I went to the corral to saddle the horses. As we headed back to town, I kept thinking about Frances instead of the trade fair. I couldn't get thoughts of her out of my head. Not that I was trying.

13 | THE TRADE FAIR

"I think you seem to like my cousin," Juan said with a laugh as we rode toward Chihuahua.

"She seems fairly perfect," I answered. "Why would I not like her? But she is beautiful and intelligent, so why would she like a wanderer like me?"

"Regardless of how you see yourself," said Juan, "she seems to see you differently. I think she is impressed by you, Bill. And she doesn't see you as a wanderer. She probably thinks of you as a trader of goods with a strong future."

I laughed and said, "If she really thinks that way, then I am about the luckiest guy in the world. What do you think her family thinks of me? Am I an adventurer or a wanderer or a businessman?"

A big smile lit up Juan's face and he said, "These days, those are all the same things. What matters most is your character and intentions. Are you a good man with strong intentions or are you a man of poor character with poor intentions? I know her family sees you as a man of high character and good intentions. That is certainly the way the rest of my family sees you too."

"So, what are you trying to tell me, Juan?"

Juan laughed again and said, "Oh, I'm not trying to tell you anything. But if you like her and she likes you, just don't let yourself think you aren't good enough for her. That's all. I wouldn't mind having you as a cousin."

I nearly choked. "A cousin? Do you think she would actually marry me?"

"Well, you might need to get to know her a little better first," Juan chuckled. "But I wouldn't entirely rule it out. Good husbands are difficult to come by. If God puts you in the right place at the right time, there is no telling what your future might hold. I guess that's what I'm saying."

"I think we are talking miracles here and it would probably take a miracle for Frances to like me that way," I said.

"Well, just don't rule it out," Juan said. "Oh, and one more thing. All the time I have known you, you act confident and business-like. I feel like you could take on the world and go up against anybody. But you get one beautiful girl involved, and suddenly you feel like you're not good enough. So, let me tell you something. You are good enough."

I laughed and told Juan thanks for his confidence. Eventually, I was finally successful in changing the subject. We talked about the trade fair and what Juan's plans were for setting up his merchandise to sell. Since the trade fair really didn't officially start until the next day, he thought we would spend time visiting with friends and other merchants to see what was going to be available. We would set up our wagons tomorrow morning.

As we neared Chihuahua, it looked like it would be a busy day. More and more merchants were flowing into town for the trade fair. In addition to our caravan from Santa Fe, there were also other groups from Santa Fe and Albuquerque. We had seen some of them on the trail and some of them we had not seen. There were also groups coming from as far south as Mexico City, and several groups coming from the port cities of

Matamoros and Tampico.

Many of the merchants were setting up shop out of their wagons. As room allowed, they were putting their wagons around the square across from the cathedral. Our caravan knew ahead of time who they were probably going to be dealing with and had already made some arrangements.

Juan and I spent most of the day walking around the group just to see what was going on and what there was for sale. The variety of merchandise was amazing. I had never been to such a large gathering of merchants. They seemed to have everything anyone would ever want. We saw most of our group scattered here and there in the crowd. There was also a large group of livestock nearby in several fenced off areas. There were cattle, sheep, goats and pigs. I suppose most of the livestock had been raised locally; although, some of the cattle appeared to have been herded here over many miles.

Late in the afternoon as business started to slow down, there was another large supper for the crowd. It was similar to what our group's families and friends had prepared for us the first evening we got to Chihuahua. Local merchants had arranged this meal. It was primarily for the traders who were selling their wares. Afterward there was a large dance in the square. It was for everybody in town. Most of the merchants who had been standing up all day just wanted to sit, relax, eat, and listen to the music.

Juan and I had used most of the time to talk to Leon and Manuel. The day was going well for both of them. Many family and friends had stopped by to see them. They had also talked business with several men they knew here in Chihuahua.

Tomorrow both of them were going to try and sell the merchandise they had brought with them. Their equipment had been set up around the plaza. Leon was going to display one of his freight wagons and see if he could sell several. Manuel was also going to set up a display showing all the items he had made to sell. Hopefully, he would be able to sell all the cast iron skillets. Also, he had a wide variety of belt buckles, bridles, harnesses, and knives he wanted to sell.

We told them about having supper and spending the night with Aunt Anita, Uncle Claudio, and their family. We also told them about Ronaldo's announcement that Luis and Lorenzo were being called into the church. As it turned out, they had heard that news already directly from Ronaldo.

And, of course, Juan had to tell them that Frances and I had eyes for each other. I told them that Juan was seeing things that weren't really there. They both laughed and said they couldn't imagine such a thing.

Leon and Manuel said they were sorry they couldn't make the supper last night. Anita and Claudio were supposed to be in town for most of the week, both at their store and attending the trade fair, so they'd catch up with them later.

Anita and Claudio were intending to buy more merchandise for their store, and also had a few items they wanted to sell. These were mainly tools and small household items that none of their customers needed.

The four of us got up and walked around the plaza a little to get away from the noise of the dancing and music that accompanied it. It was heartwarming to see people having a good time being together; but it was starting to get a little overwhelming.

It obviously was going to be an exciting time tomorrow. There were many wagons around the square, as well as smaller carts. People had brought what they wanted to sell by whatever means they had. Most of the merchants were laying out their bedrolls by their wagons or carts. Their animals were usually tied close by, so the owners could keep them fed and watered.

Some of the merchants in our caravan had joined the crowd around the square and were sleeping by their wagons also. Most of our caravan had gathered together off the square and were taking turns watching everything. Tonight, Juan and I would be taking our turn on watch. Tomorrow our group would be doing what they could to sell most or all of what they had brought. It should be a busy day.

Leon, Manuel, Juan, and I went back over to where our men were settled in and bedded down for the night. It would be a long day tomorrow.

Every man in our caravan was up early the next morning. The fresh feeling in the air promised a clear sunny day. Even though it was January, we were all hoping for a relatively warm day. There was no wind so far and that was encouraging. One of our men got a fire started and made a pot of coffee. We were all able to have a cup before the pot had to be refilled for a second round. It smelled warm and inviting. There is just something special about a cup of coffee outdoors as the sun is coming up on a beautiful day. It has always been one of my favorite things.

We were all excited about the day and started to make preparations as we finished our coffee. Juan and I moved his wagons into a good area on the side of the square. We placed his wares in a position to display and spent the first few hours seeing how the crowd developed. Later in the day, I would stay with the wagons and Juan would walk around the square seeing what he wanted to buy to take back to the trading post. He had already talked to some of the locals yesterday and knew what he would be buying from them. Some of the other things he needed would have to come from out-of-town traders.

After we had gotten the wagons ready and were about to sit down, we had a surprise. Frances and her father stopped by with breakfast.

Claudio spoke up first as they were nearing us. He said, "Frances and her mother thought you gentlemen would probably be too busy to think about eating this morning, so they made you a little something."

"That is wonderful," I said. "I really hadn't thought about

eating; but now that you've mentioned food, I'm starving."
Frances was lovely as always.

Juan said, "Me too. What did you bring us, cousin?"

Frances said, "Momma made green chili lamb and tortillas, and I made a variation of Maria's cinnamon buns that we had the other day. We thought this might help you keep up your strength."

"Thank you," I said. "That will certainly fill us up enough to get through the morning."

Juan gave them his thanks too. Then we offered them a seat and we all sat to enjoy the breakfast. The lamb and tortillas were warm and wonderful. And the buns were just like Maria had made, except there was one slight difference. I asked Frances what the difference was from Maria's buns. Frances said she likes to put a little nutmeg in hers. I told her they were really good.

I asked Frances, "What are you two doing today?"

She said, "Father is going to spend all day at his store and I am going to be there most of the day to help him. In the afternoon I will be wandering around to see what is happening at the trade fair. I might even come back to see what you two are doing."

"You are welcome back any time," I said.

"Yes, I'd say that would be a good deal," Juan added.

After a little more visiting, Frances and Claudio said they needed to get to the store and left.

The crowd had started to build up and we had talked to several other traders and locals looking for a bargain. Juan took off to do a little scouting around and I stayed with the wagons and merchandise.

We had brought a wagon full of tools that Juan had made on his forge. Friends had told me that Juan was almost as good as Manuel at a forge. After seeing his tools and knives, I could believe it. Juan also made some high-quality ropes. He enjoyed making them when he wasn't busy with something else. There were also a few flintlock rifles that Juan wanted to sell or trade for other rifles. He didn't like this kind of rifle as much as others he had seen. He also had several dozen musket type pistols. He didn't mind these; but wasn't selling as many pistols as he was rifles. It was his understanding that newer and much better pistols were coming on the market soon, so he wanted to sell these or trade them for rifles.

After a while Juan was back. He had been talking to other dealers about rifles. He wanted to take a few dozen back with us. He was reluctant to buy a large quantity all at one time, lest somebody see and want to rob us later on the trail. He talked to one dealer who would trade him rifles for pistols at the rate of three pistols for two rifles. Juan thought that was a good deal and was going to trade for six rifles. He was hoping he could find another dealer or two that would make him the same offer, so we could trade all the pistols away.

Juan stayed with the wagons for a while and I wandered around the square. I saw Carlos and Sid Poso. They were having a productive trade fair. Carlos had sold almost all the clothes he had brought with him. Also, he had made agreements with several other merchants for clothes he would take back to his store in Santa Fe. Two of the merchants were locals in Chihuahua and would hold the clothes until he was ready to go. He had taken the clothes from the other dealer and put them in the wagon already.

Sid was having fun spending time both with Carlos and a couple of attorney friends that had firms here in Chihuahua. He apparently had thought about joining with them in the past but had finally decided to stay nearer to home. They weren't from Chihuahua and had just decided it would be a good town in which to practice. They looked prosperous, so the town appeared to be treating them well.

After talking to Sid and Carlos, I decided I had better get back over to see how Juan was doing. I was glad that I went when I did. Frances was there with her beautiful smile and lovely hair. She had brought us food again. She spoke when she first saw me. "Well, it's about time you got here." She laughed. "The least you can do if a girl brings you food is show up to eat it."

"I completely agree," I said. "I was wrong. Even though I didn't know you intended to feed us again. A guy could get use to this type of treatment. We'll be heading back to Santa Fe soon. Maybe you could come with us and feed us on the trail too," I laughed.

She smiled and said, "That would be interesting, I'm sure. Maybe I'd better stay here. Aside from having the opportunity to eat meals prepared by me twice, how is your day?"

"Well, I would have to admit," I said, "that seeing you twice is the highlight of my day so far. Other than that, there have been a few other good moments. I walked around the square a while to see what kinds of merchants were here. I was amazed at the variety of dry goods and other things there were for sale. I bumped into Sid and Carlos Poso from the caravan. They were doing well. Carlos is a clothier. He had sold what he brought here to sell and had bought most of what he wanted to take back to Santa Fe. His brother Sid is an attorney in Santa Fe and just came on this trip to be with his brother and to have fun. Oh, he has seen a few friends here in Chihuahua too. Frances, how has your day been?"

"It's been nice," Frances said. "I worked with my father in his store. He has been especially busy today with customers brought in by the trade fair. I helped him a little and then spent some time with Momma over at the house. Now, I'm going to go check on the store for a while and then go spend some more time at the house. You two are invited for supper. Just come over when things start to shut down here."

"I don't know where your house is," I said.

"You had better learn then," she said. "Juan can show you

the way. Oh, I think Leon and Manuel and some of their friends will be there too. I don't know what we will have, but Momma is a pretty good cook." She whirled around and headed west.

I watched her walk away. She was wearing a long wool skirt, a white long-sleeved blouse, a light-colored leather belt and a burgundy vest. She was as attractive a woman as I had ever met. And she seemed to like me. I was thinking that Chihuahua was a wonderful place.

Juan and I stayed with the wagon until it started to get dark. Part of our group would be watching the wagons, equipment, and horses for the evening. Several of the rest of us would relieve them later.

We cleaned up a bit and then headed over to Frances's house. Manuel and Santiago were already there, as were Leon and Alberto. They said the other four would be along soon. Everyone was drinking beer that Claudio had made. Juan and I felt compelled to join in with the beer drinking. Claudio was a good beer maker. His beer was dark and smooth. I think I had something similar in New Orleans.

The group talked about how things at the trade fair had gone for them. Leon and Alberto had a spectacular day. Alberto said, "We sold two wagons and took orders for six more. Hopefully we can take some additional wagon orders tomorrow. That would keep us busy all spring."

People liked their wagons because they were built strong and had a system using flat metal slats as springs that gave the wagons a good ride. And, from my personal experience of this past month, I thought that was an excellent idea.

Manuel and Santiago had an excellent day also. Manuel said, "We sold almost all of our cast iron skillets, since they are unique. And we sold almost half of our belt buckles, bridles, and harnesses. The leather goods and knives went really quick this morning too. I don't think we have any left. It was a good day. Don't you think Santiago?"

"I do indeed," he said. "I've never seen anything quite like it."

Juan said, "It was a good day for us as well. We sold about two thirds of our tools and knives. I brought a few flintlock rifles to sell. I sold them first thing this morning. And I traded for some other rifles with pistols I didn't need. Tomorrow I need to start buying trapping equipment to replenish my supply back home."

About that time the rest of the group showed up. It was Jaime, Antonio, Jose and Diego, the friends Leon had invited along to Chihuahua as spare drivers. They had spent the day visiting old friends and family. They were not related to Juan's family. Their families had always lived close to one another in Chihuahua when they were younger.

Claudio let everybody know that supper was ready. All the food was set up on the counter near the dining table. Everyone served themselves and ate wherever they liked, since we couldn't all fit at the dining table.

Frances got in line by me and suggested we go out back to the patio where there was a small table. It was quiet and comfortable, a good place for a conversation.

Frances sat down by my side and asked, "Bill, what do you think of Chihuahua?"

"I think it is beautiful and a nice place to live," I said. "It is busy and industrious. The architecture is attractive, and the plants are new and impressive to me. I have been enjoying the trade fair. And it has been a pleasure to meet you and your family. I know it is your hometown. After having been away to Mexico City for several years, what do you think of Chihuahua?"

"I don't know really," she said. "It is not Mexico City. I think this is a good place to live. I enjoyed growing up here. Chihuahua and Mexico City are the only places I have ever lived. I'm glad you like it here. You are the one with all of the experience traveling, so, if you think it is nice, I'm glad about that."

"Most of my experience traveling," I said, "is across country alone. Other than New Orleans, Santa Fe, Albuquerque, and Chihuahua, most of what I have seen are towns with only a few hundred people in them. You seem to think I have traveled a lot, but I haven't really. Troy is the traveler. He is the one that sailed with Juan to many ports along the Atlantic Ocean. I'll be heading to St. Louis in the spring, and then onto New Orleans. I'd ask you to go with me, but it will be dangerous."

She said, "I'm sure that would be fun. I might have a hard time getting my parents to agree to a trip like that. Maybe you could stay here in Chihuahua and start a business or work with my father? I'm sure he could use you."

"I would enjoy that a great deal," I said. "But, I'm obligated to get back in touch with Troy and tell him all I have found out about the dry goods business in Santa Fe, Albuquerque, and Chihuahua. That is the reason that I came here in the first place. I wish I could just click my fingers and go back there to see him. Then I could click my fingers again and come back here."

"I would like that," she said with an intriguing smile.

Frances and I had just about forgotten to eat our meals. We finished them and went back for dessert. Our dessert was eaten in the swing on the front porch. We talked and talked and talked. I didn't really know what to do. I wanted to stay here near Frances; but I was obligated to get back with Troy. There was time to think about it. We probably wouldn't leave for another week. I felt pretty sure I knew what I had to do and that made me sad.

Juan came out of the house after a while and suggested we head back to the square. I squeezed Frances's hand and got up. I told her I would see her some time tomorrow.

Frances got up and said, "You two are not leaving without a hug." She hugged Juan and then hugged me especially warmly, I thought.

"Hey, you can bring us breakfast again in the morning if you don't have any other plans," I said jokingly.

"I don't know what I'll need to do in the morning," she said with a serious look on her face. "But I'll think about it."

We told her good night and headed back to the square.

At first light in the morning, we were up getting organized. By tonight, we would probably get the last of Juan's merchandise sold. And hopefully he would finish buying all the things needed to take back to the trading post for his customers. It also sounded like most of our group would be in the same shape that we were. Once all the men in our caravan were finished with business at the trade fair, everyone was still planning to stay in Chihuahua for four or five more days. Of course that could change, if the other group from our caravan needed to get home quicker. We didn't anticipate that though. Juan was going to talk to Pablo first thing this morning to see when they might want to leave.

By the time we were ready for the crowd of buyers and sellers to start milling around, Juan and I were starting to get hungry. Just then we were visited by a beautiful angel from the west, the west side of the square that is. It was Frances. She had her beautiful black hair pulled back into a ponytail and she was wearing another riding outfit. She brought us some food that smelled strongly of cinnamon, oregano, cumin, and coffee.

"How would you guys like some pork chili with tortillas, cinnamon buns, and coffee?"

"That would be perfect," I offered. "Don't you think so, Juan?"

He laughed and said, "I agree. It would be perfect."

Juan started with a cinnamon bun and so did I. We both were attracted to sweets for breakfast; but that would not keep us from finishing the pork chili. The food was eaten quickly because customers were starting to look around at what Juan still had left to sell. Frances visited with us for a few minutes and then headed to her father's store. She was intending to help him for most of the day. I told her I would stop by later to see how she was doing. Juan and I were going to trade off staying by the wagon for the morning.

I stayed with the wagon first while Juan went out both to see Pablo and to walk around the square. He wanted to see what deals he might make. The crowd built up slower than the day before. Everyone seemed to be getting tired after several days of work and getting together with friends and family. I could see why. Frances helped me forget about my own fatigue.

Sid Poso stopped by the wagon to visit. Sid was an interesting guy. He had traveled a lot when he was younger, just like Juan and Troy. After going to school in Mexico City, he had seen most of Mexico. Sid had traveled as far south as the Yucatan and finally settled down in Santa Fe to open a law office. He settled in Santa Fe because he had more friends and family there than anywhere else. Sid said he had been having a great time in Chihuahua with friends, family, and business associates. We had a short visit and then he was off to see some others from our caravan.

Juan came back after an hour or so. He had talked to Pablo, the leader of the other group from our caravan. Pablo thought their group was thinking like our group on when we should leave. So, we were going to be in Chihuahua for another five or six days. That sounded good to me. I really wanted to spend more time with Frances and her family.

While Juan was away, I had sold some more hand tools and all the remaining knives. We were almost finished selling the goods we had brought to Chihuahua. Juan still needed a few more items he had just remembered. That would complete everything he needed to do at the trade fair. He was going to get those purchases finished this afternoon.

I stayed with Juan and visited with other traders as they came by until late in the morning. Then I went over to Claudio and Anita's store. Frances and Josepha were both at the house cooking with their mother. I talked to Claudio for a while. He had been unusually busy for the past few days because of the big crowd in town. The crowd this morning had slowed down as it got closer to lunch. He was at the store by himself now. Frances, Josepha and Anita had all been there earlier to help. They had gone to the house when business slowed down.

Claudio was telling me that he started his store first and built the house in town. When the store got successful, they bought some land outside town to start their rancho. They had lived out there most of the time that their children were growing up. They liked both being in town close to friends and on their rancho where they could relax and enjoy life at a different pace.

Claudio said, "My parents grew up in Spain and had been merchants there. At some point they decided they would like the adventure of moving to Mexico. They sailed here with a ship load of settlers from the port at Valencia. They landed in Veracruz and eventually made their way up to Chihuahua after a couple of years. There were other relatives on the same ship as theirs. Some of them stayed near Mexico City and rest of them came to Chihuahua. Some of them eventually moved to Santa Fe; but that was many years later. That is why we are scattered out. It is nice to have a large family. Anita and I were already married and came over here with my parents. Anita's parents also came in the same group of settlers. We still have family and friends in Spain. I am afraid we do not communicate with them well enough."

"Yes, it is nice to have a large family," I said. "I used to think that I had a large family, but yours is much larger than mine. I need to get back to Alabama some day and see my sisters and brothers. Of course, they are a little scattered out by now too."

About that time Frances and Josepha came in carrying a pot of chili with beef and a basket of flat bread made with corn meal. They gave some of each to Claudio, and then suggested we carry the rest over to where Juan was.

We found Juan talking to Manuel and Leon. Everyone dug

out a bowl from their wagon supplies and we ate together. The chili and flat bread were warm and filling. We sat and talked about how the day was going. Almost everything that we had intended to sell had been sold. So, we were essentially finished with the trade fair.

All of us from the caravan would need to make arrangements with each other for guarding the wagons until we were ready to leave in about a week; but that wouldn't be difficult. We had been doing that for the entire trip.

Juan said he would close down the wagon. He was going to gather up the additional rifles he had traded for and get them loaded in the wagon. The other wagon was entirely filled with trapping supplies to take back to the trading post. I told him I would be back in a little while and help him with that.

Josepha was taking the pan back to their house. Frances and I decided we would circle the square again to see how everything was going with what remained of the trade fair. Then I would head back to the wagons to help Juan finish up.

Frances and I had a slow walk around the square talking to people we knew and also to some who we were meeting for the first time. It was a beautiful day. The sun was shining and it was comfortably warm. Many birds were around and made it feel like spring. There was a mix of people from all over the Mexico on the square. They were selling an unbelievable assortment of goods.

The trade fair had slowed down considerably in some respects; but was busier in others. Some traders had gotten to Chihuahua late and were doing their best to get their merchandise sold before everyone packed up to go home.

The latest arriving traders had come from Mexico City. They did not get started when they intended because of heavy rain. Even though it was January, Chihuahua had been fairly warm. Mexico City was 900 miles to the south, so it was always warm there.

We were all wondering what the weather would be like when we returned to Santa Fe. It could be fairly comfortable like it had been when we came south to Chihuahua or it could be cold and snowing. I was certainly hoping for good weather.

Frances and I talked about the trade fair, the beautiful day, our families, old friends and our childhoods. It was one of those days when you are happy to be alive and feel like you are in the perfect place with the perfect person and that perfect person feels the same way that you do. But then something always happens to bring you back to reality.

Frances asked, "Bill, when will your caravan go back to Santa Fe?"

I wasn't sure if I wanted to go back to Santa Fe. It was too pleasant here in Chihuahua. At that moment only one thing would have taken me back to Santa Fe and on to the U.S. and that was obligation. I knew I was obligated to go back to New Orleans and tell Troy what I had found out on my trip to Santa Fe.

"I think we are all figuring on a week more here and then we will leave," I said. "Most of the men in our group have been so busy that they haven't had time to enjoy Chihuahua or spend time with their relatives. It seems that most of them have relatives here. Thankfully, they would all like more time here before we leave. I hope that you and I can spend some more time together."

"I would like that too," she said. "Will you have to do any more work before you leave?"

"Everyone in our group will share guard duty over the wagons while we are still here," I said. "And I will be helping Juan more this afternoon to get some things loaded. Aside from that I'm not obligated to do anything in particular except be available, if I am needed. What will you be doing for the next week?"

"I thought you might enjoy seeing the rest of Chihuahua," Frances said. "There are some other areas I would like to show you, when you can get away."

"I'd love to anytime," I said. "We could get together in the morning and spend as much time as you want. Would that work? Have you got any obligations at school in the next week?"

"That would work fine," she said. "I don't have any obligations at school for the next ten days. The school is on mid-winter break. Why don't you come over to the house for breakfast in the morning? We will eat breakfast with my parents and then ride around town. We will take a picnic lunch and come back in the afternoon."

"That sounds great," I said. "I will look forward to it. I understand there will be another meal and dance here on the square tonight. Will you be here?"

"Yes, my parents and I are intending to come," Frances said with a smile. "We'll see you at the supper."

"I'll see you then," I said. Frances headed back to her house and I went to find Juan.

14 | FAREWELL TO CHIHUAHUA

I found Juan talking to some of our group. Everyone was finished with what they had come to Chihuahua to do. They had all done well. Now it was just a matter of getting back to Santa Fe.

I was thinking the trip would take less time going home than it did coming to Chihuahua. We all knew what to expect this time. We would all be on the lookout for problems. There had been no recent rumors of possible problems along the trail. We would certainly be cautious anyway.

Before we left though, everyone wanted to relax and enjoy Chihuahua. The trade fair would continue for several more days; but it was getting smaller, and for our group it was over.

Juan and I finished loading the wagons. Pablo and Juan had found an area near the square where we could keep all the wagons and animals together, just like we had on the trail. They set up a rotation for guard duty. Then everyone got ready for the meal and dance. I thought most of us would eat and relax instead of dancing.

When we got to the meal, the largest crowd so far was in attendance. All the traders who had been working at the fair were there, as far as I could tell. Our entire caravan was there also and most of their friends and relatives.

Frances said that she and her mother and father would be at the meal, so I was looking for them. Juan and I had been sitting off to the side talking to two men we hadn't met until today. After we had been there about a half hour, I saw Frances and her parents walking through the crowd. Frances was in a lovely light blue dress with a long flowing skirt. She usually wore riding clothes, so this was different than what I had seen her in before. She was more stunning than ever. I had my newest shirt and slacks on, but I was way underdressed compared to her. Thank goodness most of the traders at supper had had a hard day standing on the square by their wagons, and they made me look good.

I greeted Frances and her family. Then we moved over to the supper line. It was a basic meal this time; but there was plenty of it. We all got some beans and tortillas, lamb chili, and an empanada. There was water to drink. We moved over to a quiet area closer to the cathedral to eat.

Josepha was coming to the dance with some friends but wasn't coming to the supper. Since she had just finished school in Chihuahua, all her friends were still in the area. But many of Frances's friends had married and settled down or had moved away.

I told Anita and Claudio that our group was finished with what they wanted to do at the trade fair. I explained that most of them, like Juan, Manuel, and Leon, all had family and friends in the area. I said we would all probably leave in five or six days to head back to Santa Fe.

Frances smiled and said, "Well, there are several more things you need to see before you leave. In fact, we should make a list. Of course, we will see more of Chihuahua tomorrow, like we have planned. The next day we need to go to the Nombre de Dios Caves just outside town on the east side. It is a large system of caves that people have investigated with special equipment. We will be able to see only a portion of it since we don't have any equipment for descending into the main cave. But you'll find it fascinating. It is cooler in the cave, and it is filled with unusual structures that grow from the caves' floors or ceilings or both. I love it there. I'm sure you will also."

"I would especially love to see the caves," Bill said. "In Alabama, near where we lived, were some caves that I went in once. It was amazing how they looked on the inside. Water had obviously cut them out over thousands of years. I didn't see any unusual structures like you mentioned; but just the size was very impressive."

"Then we will have to think about what to do the next day." Frances continued. "Ah, let me think. Oh yes, we need to ride out five miles or so into Pequis Canyon. It's really beautiful. The variety of plants is spectacular. And the dimensions of the valley and the height of the canyon walls in general is surprising. It goes all the way to Ojinaga, so we won't be able to see but a little of it. You'll like it though and I'll make a picnic lunch."

"Sounds good to me," I said. "I would like to do anything with you."

"Yes, I know," she said with a giggle. "But as long as you are here, you might as well see some of the things that make this area special."

"I'd love to," I said.

The music had started, and we saw Josepha and her friends starting to dance. I wasn't sure if I felt much like dancing; but, when Frances suggested we dance, I couldn't refuse. We excused ourselves from where we were sitting with her parents and moved toward the crowd. The music was rather fast at first. I suppose that was to get the people excited about getting up from their seats. We whirled around and I danced with all the rhythm there was in me. It was fun being with Frances. Dancing is something I had never thought I would like, but with Frances I felt I could do it forever.

As the music eventually slowed down and the rhythm changed, Frances and I danced closer together. I held Frances in my arms as we moved with the crowd. Dancing with her was so special, I could barely stand it. I knew I was falling in love with her. And I think she was falling in love with me. I didn't know how our lives would work out so we could be together, but I knew that she was the one for me.

Eventually the crowd got smaller as people started to leave. We finally sat down again. Anita and Claudio had left for home already. We talked to Juan, Manuel, and Leon. We told them about our plans for the next three days. They thought the plans sounded good. They had all seen most of Chihuahua in the past as well as Pequis Canyon. I few of them had seen a little of the caves and thought they were worth seeing.

We excused ourselves and I walked Frances home. I needed to get back to the wagons for guard duty soon.

Frances said, "If you will come over to our house in the morning, I will fix you breakfast. And I will fix a sack lunch to take on our adventure around town. First, I have arranged with Ronaldo to give us a tour of the cathedral. You will enjoy that. It is gorgeous. Then I'm not sure what route we will take after that, but there is a lot to see."

We had just gotten to Frances's house. I said, "I am really looking forward to seeing your city with you. It sounds like a lot of fun. I'll see you for breakfast."

I was starting to leave when she took my arm and moved closer to me. She leaned in and kissed me. I kissed her back... for a while. I didn't want to leave but knew I needed to. I told her I would see her in the morning.

The rest of the evening, my guard duty and sleep passed

quickly. I was tired from all we had done that day and went to sleep easily when guard duty was over.

When I walked up onto the porch at Frances's house, I could smell breakfast cooking. Claudio met me at the front door. He was just leaving for work at the store. He smiled at me and shook my hand. He said, "Bill, it is nice to see you. Frances tells me she is going to show you Chihuahua today. I hope you enjoy it. We feel it is a beautiful and friendly place to live."

I said, "Thanks. From all I have seen, Chihuahua is a good town to live in. I hope you have a good day at the store."

Claudio said, "Oh, Frances asked me to tell you to go around back to the porch. She was going to set you a cup of coffee there. See you soon."

I walked around back by a pathway from the front porch. They had many succulent plants in a beautiful setting all along the side and back of the house. Even though it was January, it seemed to always be warm enough for these plants to grow.

I sat down at the table on the porch where Frances had set a large mug of coffee. The coffee was dark and strong, not bitter. It was almost like my chicory coffee. Unfortunately, I had run out of the chicory coffee months ago back at the trading post.

Frances brought out a platter of beans, tortillas, and pork for us to share. She said, "I thought we could enjoy this together. It will be quick and then we can be on our way."

It was warm and comforting. We finished off the meal with vanilla scented cake and more coffee.

Frances said, "I told Ronaldo that we would be at the cathedral early, so that we can get a good start to the day."

I thanked Frances for her wonderful meal and we both headed off to see Ronaldo and the cathedral.

It was a crisp morning with absolutely no wind, so it was beautiful walking from the house to the cathedral. Of course, we had to walk by the plaza, so we got to see how things were going there. Some traders were still working at buying and selling, but the crowd had gotten much smaller. Other traders were busy starting to pack up for home, wherever that happened to be. Most of us had many miles to go before we were home. That was especially true for me since I was considering New Orleans currently as home. Santa Fe was certainly starting to feel like home too. And Chihuahua obviously has its treasures also. I could easily see Chihuahua as home.

Ronaldo met us at a side door to the cathedral. He said, "Good morning. It is so nice to see you both this morning." He hugged Frances and shook my hand. "Bill, I am so glad that Frances asked me to show you the cathedral. It is so beautiful and I love it here. I hope you will really enjoy it. Please come in and let's get started. Frances told me you have a full day of touring around town planned."

We entered almost immediately into a small side chapel. It was beautiful with lovely woodwork and several detailed paintings. Ronaldo continued, "The Church of Saint Francis of Assisi was started in the early 1700's and finished about 1792; however, it is still constantly being worked on and may never be complete." As we walked into the central part of the church, he said "This is the nave. It was one of the first parts of the cathedral to be built. I think it is especially lovely." As we walked toward the front of the nave, he lowered his voice because there were several people there praying. "The chancel is also a beautiful and special place. Most of us in the cathedral spend several hours each day here." We quietly walked through the nave and chancel. The ceiling overhead was massive.

As we moved into a hall off to the side of the chancel, Ronaldo said, "You probably noticed the columns in front of the cathedral. They were built in a style not widely used in Spain at the time, so they are unique. The cathedral was designed in what they call the Spanish Baroque style. It was built in the form of a cross. There is a huge dome above the crossing. The cathedral officially sits on the Plaza de Armas and is considered to be one of the loveliest buildings in all of Mexico."

I said, "Ronaldo, it is lovely. Thank you so much for letting us see it this morning."

"It is my pleasure, Bill," Ronaldo said. "Thank you for coming to see it."

It was amazingly beautiful. I had never seen anything quite like it. I had been in the cathedral at Santa Fe and that was certainly lovely too. The cathedral gave me an overwhelming sense of peace and beauty. I loved being with Frances and her brother here. It was truly a perfect way to start the day.

As we were finishing our tour, Ronaldo took us into a small parlor and gave us some tea and biscuits. We sat and talked a while about Chihuahua and how they enjoyed growing up there. The population was over 4,000 citizens now, and even though it wasn't large by city standards, they loved it.

I told Ronaldo again how much I enjoyed seeing the cathedral and what a beautiful place I thought it was. Frances and I wished him a good day and then continued our tour of Chihuahua.

First, we headed toward an impressive government building nearby. Originally, it had been a Jesuit College. It was converted into a military hospital in 1790. Around this area were several other buildings that held various government functions. They were all surrounded by several dozen large trees. There were also stores of a variety of types and some fine residences.

We went by another beautiful church and Frances wanted to stop. She said, "Bill, I love this church too. It is the Temple of St. Francisco. It's not as large as the cathedral. I have always thought it was impressive too with its high ceilings and marble floors and archways. It was started in the early 1700's and finished in the late 1700's. My family attended this church when I was small.

We didn't have an invitation for a tour of this church. We walked in the front door and looked around a minute. Then we went to find a small park where Frances played when she was a little girl. Frances had brought a small picnic lunch and we shared it there. The park was covered with trees and shrubs and with the occasional open space for picnics and playing. The sun was shining and there was no wind. Birds were singing, but we didn't see them flying around. We ate our lunch and talked for a long time about when we were children growing up.

I told Frances about growing up in Alabama with seven other siblings and my mother and father. I told her about how my parents met, gotten married and settled down in eastern Alabama to farm.

We talked about our siblings. Of course, I knew her siblings and what they were doing. She didn't know much about mine. We had talked about them briefly before, but not in any detail. Now I told her everything of interest I could think of. She knew about Troy, so I told her about my other two brothers, Aubrey and Donald, that farm together back home. Then I told her about my four sisters, Jo Beth, Onita, Willa and Janette, that are married to farmers in the same area.

Frances told me stories she had heard about her mother and father and their parents. She told me about their immigration to this area and their building a life here.

After our lunch we walked along a stream that meandered through the park. It was a peaceful place. It made the world seem perfect. And, I would have to admit that at the moment, my life was just about perfect.

It was easy to see why Frances loved her hometown so much. It was a special place.

We walked for a long time and then circled back around to see a little more of the town. After that we went back to Frances' house. She invited me in for supper with her mother and father. We had a good time talking about their family and their immigration from Spain. We had talked about it before; but every time I heard the stories, they were exciting. I loved the thought of going from one part of the world to another. Making a life in a new world sounded like a great adventure. I guess I had been having a new adventure ever since I left New Orleans for Mexico. It had certainly been fun. And now I had met a woman that was making me want to stay here and settle down. I needed to go back to New Orleans. How could I just leave Frances here? But then again, how could I take her away from this area and her family that she loves?

Anita asked me to spend the night in Ronaldo's bedroom instead of going back to the caravan. I didn't have guard duty, so I said I would love to.

Frances and I talked a while longer in the living room and then she showed me where Ronaldo's bedroom was. We kissed goodnight. I told her to have sweet dreams. She said she would dream about me.

I woke up early and started getting dressed. Frances and I were going to Nombre de Dios (Name of God) caves and that sounded interesting. I knew we were only going to see a little of the caves. You needed special gear to access the biggest parts of the cave. We apparently would follow a stream inside from higher up on a hill, above the larger entrance. That would allow us to see some of the unique features of the cave.

As I was finishing getting ready, I heard Anita knock softly on the door and say that the coffee was ready.

Frances and I got to the kitchen table at about the same time. We smiled at each other as we sat down. I had never seen such a beautiful smile. It was like a valley after a rain with beautiful clouds overhead and sunbeams coming down from behind them.

Anita brought us both cups of coffee and sweet buns to start with. That was followed by a tamale dish that was new to me and especially good. We both had a couple cups of coffee and two helpings of Anita's tamale dish. We talked to Anita a bit, thanked her for breakfast, and then headed out for the day's adventure.

The caves were not more than a mile or two out of town on the east side of town. Our route missed the square, so we didn't see what activity was going on with the remnants of the trade fair. We did see a portion of town that I had not seen. It was mostly residences and then a rural homestead or two. As we left town the elevation of the land began to increase. We were moving into a hilly area. However, the trail leading to the caves was well traveled and lined by attractive native plants. They all seemed to be succulent plants similar to ones I had seen near the rancho. We saw two coyotes, a fox, and more birds than I could count. It was a beautiful ride that took only about twenty minutes.

As we got to the area where the caves were, the hills got rockier and their tops higher. Frances first showed me the entrance to the main cave that required special equipment to descend into. It looked, at first, like a small opening into the hill. Then it became obvious that the opening went only about fifty feet forward into the hill. Most of the opening went down at a steep angle. It was far too steep to walk down into. It wasn't really straight down, but it was close enough to make climbing down dangerous. From the main opening you could see some of the special sights in the cave. I'm sure it was really spectacular farther inside. We spent a little time around the cave entrance enjoying the scenery.

Then we rode the horses east away from the main opening until we found a trail that went up a hill about a half mile. There we found a grove of trees with a little clearing in the middle. Going through the clearing, we found a stream that apparently came from a spring farther up the hill. The stream went through the trees and into a small cave opening. It appeared that we were almost directly over the main entrance.

Frances had brought a torch smeared on one end with an oily substance over some cloth. She said a torch would be necessary for us to see inside the cave. I lit the torch with a spark from flint and steel that I always kept in my saddle bags.

As we walked into the opening, the temperature seemed to get warmer after we had gone no more than twenty feet. The path was going generally downhill. I assumed it might eventually lead to the cave below unless there was an obstruction of some kind in the way.

Even though this area was supposedly much smaller than the main cave below, it still seemed amazingly big to me. The scale of it was larger than anything I had ever seen underground. Back in Alabama I had been in caves big enough for a small family to shelter in during a storm; but that was the extent of my cave exploration. This was something vastly different.

Soon we began to see unusual rock formations that looked unreal. Most of them were like columns either coming up from the floor or hanging from the ceiling. They were usually wet. The water must have been seeping in from water collected in rock layers above when it rained.

The torch lit up the walls enough that colors of rock could be seen. Some areas were a solid tan color; but other areas showed veins of red, brown, purple and cream also. It was extremely picturesque. I could imagine artists spending days here painting picture after picture.

"Frances, what are we seeing here?" I asked. "I have never seen anything like this."

"I'm not sure what they are called," said Frances, "but I know how they are supposedly formed. Apparently, the water seeping in from springs above dissolves some of the limestone and it gets redeposited below in the form of these strange-shaped formations. It is all really beautiful, don't you think?"

"Yes," I said. "I wouldn't have thought that such a thing was even possible. How many times have you been in here before?"

"My family enjoys this area," she said. "I have been here many times. The cave continues for a while, then it stops where there are some rocks that are much harder than the limestone.

It was not dissolved away. The path ends there but the water continues to seep farther down. I assume it is what creates the bottom cavern and forms the unusual formations that are also down there. There is a much larger space there and many times more formations."

We continued on until we could go no further. At that point we decided to sit down and enjoy the sights. After twenty minutes or so, Frances began to worry that the torch might burn out. She said that it was so dark here with no light, that finding our way out to daylight would be difficult. We got back to the cave entrance as the torch was getting weak and finally burned out.

When we were back out of the cave and with the horses, we decided it was time to eat our picnic lunch that Anita had so kindly packed for us. She had packed dried fruit, bread and cheese. It was filling and enjoyable.

We talked about some of the trips her family had been on to this area. She said that Ronaldo had gone into the larger part of the cave with some people with special equipment. Even after visiting here many times, he was amazed by the bigger cave. He said that eventually someone needs to create an easy way to get into the bigger area. He said many people would come here and pay money to see it. She hoped that he was right. I know I would love to see it.

It began to look a little stormy, so we rode back into town. We went to Frances's house for supper. It was wonderful, as usual. We talked about our day for several hours with Frances' parents. They told me some of their favorite times there. And they told me about how much Ronaldo had enjoyed going into the cavern. They felt that being overwhelmed with God's creation may have moved his thoughts further toward serving the church.

After supper I told Frances that I needed to go back to the caravan to spend the night. I knew that I had guard duty and wanted to see how everyone was doing. We visited a while longer. We kissed good night with a long embrace. She told me she would bring me breakfast in the morning. I told her I looked forward to seeing her in the morning and took off toward the square.

At our camp site near the square, I visited with Juan and the rest of the group. Everyone was thinking it was about time to go home. They thought that we should spend one more day here and then head north to Santa Fe and their families.

Frances and I were thinking we might have a couple more days, but that had been cut to one. I would tell her in the morning. We were planning to go to El Peguis Canyon. It wouldn't be a long ride since we didn't intend to go far. Frances said it would be a beautiful ride even though it was winter. She said I should see it sometime in the spring or fall.

I was still torn as to what I should do. I knew the right thing to do was to go back to see Troy and tell him what I had learned. But my heart wanted to have the caravan go back to Santa Fe without me.

I knew that I loved Frances and I was pretty sure that she loved me too. But I didn't see how I could ask her to wait for me for what may be a year. It didn't seem right to ask her to do that.

It was good that I had middle of the night guard duty because I couldn't sleep anyway. However, by the time guard duty was over, I was able to relax and sleep for a few hours before the sun started coming up.

I told Juan some of my thoughts over a cup of coffee he had made for us.

He whistled and finally said, "Wow, that is a decision, isn't it?" He laughed and said, "Well I'd still like to have you as a cousin, but I know you want to do what is right with Troy. If it just wasn't so far to New Orleans, things could work out much better and quicker."

About that time Frances rode up with a basket of rolls, some lamb, and coffee. As always, she looked gorgeous in her riding outfit. Today she was wearing tan split skirt pants and a sky-blue blouse along with a broad brimmed straw hat. Frances hugged Juan and told him that she was certainly glad that he had come to the trade fair. He laughed and said he was too.

We sat and talked a while over our breakfast. Juan told Frances how the group had decided that we should leave for home tomorrow. She was a little shocked, but not completely surprised. She told Juan that we were going on a ride out into El Peguis Canyon.

Juan said, "That should be beautiful. I haven't ridden through the canyon for a long time. I want to do that the next time I come here. I need to go visit with Pablo about our trip tomorrow. He is the leader of the other group we are traveling with. So, if you two will excuse me, I'd better go catch him before he gets busy with his day. Frances, it has been so good to see you. I hope you and your parents will come see us off in the morning. Oh, and please thank Anita for the breakfast." He hugged her and headed off toward the other end of our group of wagons.

Frances and I walked over to where I had Morgan picketed. I saddled him and we walked him back to her horse.

As we mounted, Frances said, "Let's ride back to my house for a minute. I want to tell my parents that your group will be leaving in the morning." She had sadness in her voice. I thought for a minute she was going to cry.

When we got to her house, Frances said, "Bill, why don't you wait here with the horses, and I'll go tell my parents. I'll be right back."

Frances seemed to be gone much longer than I expected and when she came back her eyes were red. She said, "My parents said they will come see the caravan off in the morning. They were sorry to hear that everyone is leaving so soon."

We mounted up and headed east out of town. The start of the canyon was only a mile or so from the edge of town. At this point it was more like a wide valley than a canyon. She said that farther down it seemed more like a canyon when the walls grew higher and higher.

The wide valley was striking in its size. The stream we rode along was filled with colorful gravel laying over dark red sandstone. It flowed like a snake curving this way, and then that way, along the canyon floor. The variety of plants was overwhelming. I had never seen many of them before, but they were all amazing. The colors were spectacular. I assumed the colors were much more vibrant in the summer. Most of the plants were desert loving plants, so that's why I had never seen them. Coming across the prairie after leaving Louisiana was as near as I had ever come to a desert.

As we rode along, Frances said, "My family has always enjoyed riding out here. It goes on for miles and is beautiful the entire way to Ojinaga. We won't ride nearly that far today, of course. I thought we could ride until we decide to eat lunch. Then we could stop for a while, eat lunch, and head back."

We rode along slowly enjoying the beauty. I was thinking about needing to leave and not wanting to. I'm sure she was thinking of something similar.

There was a spring along the way where water ran down over red rocks that were round, shiny and rather unusual looking. The water collected in a natural basin. We watered the horses there and moved on down the trail. We rode along for several more miles until we found a clearing to stop at for lunch. The horses were picketed by the stream that flowed through the canyon.

We ate lunch and talked. Both of us were trying to maintain a brave face, but we were on the verge of tears.

Finally, Frances said, "Bill, I don't want you to leave. I know you have got to go back to see Troy. And I know that it will take a long time. Bill, I have fallen in love with you, and I think you love me too. I wish that I could go with you, but I really can't leave now. There would be nobody else to teach some of the classes I am going to teach at the cathedral. I do hope and pray that you will come back as soon as you can. I would love to make a life with you."

I said, "Frances, I love you too. And I also hope that we can make a life together." We kissed and cried and hugged for a long time.

Then we saddled up and headed back toward Chihuahua. We rode so close to each other that we could practically hold hands.

It was a beautiful day, a wonderful day, and a sad day all at the same time. We had both expressed our love for each other. Still, I was going away. However, I was sure of one thing. I would do everything I could to get back to Frances as soon as possible. I told her that. And with every bit of my heart, I meant it.

When we got back to Chihuahua, we stopped by Frances's house. She said that she and her family would come by about supper time and bring some supper. I held her in my arms for a long time. We kissed and I headed back to our camp.

I talked to Juan when I got back to camp. I told him of our promises to each other. I also told him of my intention to leave as soon as we got back to the trading post. He congratulated me and said he would miss me once I headed back to the U.S.

Juan and I spent some time making sure that we were ready to go. The rest of our caravan was ready to leave.

We all seemed set to leave this place that had become so magical to me. It would be a quick trip back to Santa Fe. However, we all fully intended to be vigilant and cautious on this return trip. None of us wanted anything along the way to cause problems or slow down the trip.

It was about time to start thinking about supper, when Frances, Anita, and Claudio came by to see us. They had a large pot of beef chili for our entire group. We sat around and talked for a while. They said they enjoyed us being there. We told them we enjoyed it as well, more than we could ever really express. Their intentions were to be back in the morning to see us off.

Frances and I walked away from the group about fifty feet. We kissed and hugged each other warmly. She said she would see me in the morning. Then we walked back over to the group. She and her mother and father gave us a warm good evening and then headed for home.

I stayed up late for another round of guard duty. When I finished with my duty and went to bed, I found that my mind was too full of Frances and her family to go to sleep. I spent the rest of the night thinking.

I got up when activity started around camp. We intended to start as soon as the sun was up, if we could. I got Morgan ready to go. Juan got Red saddled and helped me with the mules. As the other teams got hooked up and ready to go, we moved into position to head out toward Santa Fe.

When we were close to being ready to leave, Frances and her parents came by. They gave us some food to eat this morning on the way. There were tortillas rolled around pork and cinnamon buns. It was good that Juan had been thinking about provisions for us, and food and water for the animals, because I certainly hadn't. My mind seemed to be barely moving. I could only think of one thing, and I was soon to ride away from her. I had no idea when I would be able to see her again, and it hurt down inside. I could hardly move. But I knew that I had to move, and keep moving, to get to New Orleans and back to Chihuahua. It was the most important thing I had ever done. And I would do it. With every fiber of my being, I would do it.

Juan and Pablo decided it was time to go and that word went up and down the line.

Anita and Claudio each gave me a big hug and said they looked forward to my return.

Frances and I moved away from the caravan for a few minutes. We looked at each other and kissed warmly. I whispered to her I wasn't sure how I could stand to be without her. I promised

I would hurry back as soon as I could. I said that I had calculated that I would hopefully be back by late summer. I told her I loved her and would have her in my heart and mind every day. She said she loved me with all her heart and would think of me constantly until I got back. We kissed again and held each other tight as tears rolled down our cheeks.

She walked me over to the wagon and we kissed goodbye. We both said, "I'll see you in late summer. I love you."

I got in my wagon and picked up the reigns. Frances and I were looking at each other. We both raised our hand to our mouths and blew each other a kiss.

At almost that very moment, Juan yelled, and the caravan started moving forward. All the noise and activity couldn't take my attention away from Frances or my thoughts away from the long journey ahead.

The End

Other Books by the Author

The Rampy Family series, Book 2
TRAIL to NEW ORLEANS

The Rampy Family series, Book 3
TRAIL to HOME

Made in the USA
Columbia, SC
10 June 2025

59222808R00109